Murphy's Bridge to Life

Murphy's Bridge to Life

Mr. Albert Earl

Dedication

*I would like to first dedicate this book to my **wife, Maria Rodriguez**, who has been there for me in all aspects of support. Even when I was dealing with my internal demons, when most significant others or partners in a relationship might feel like it was too much of a task to deal with me, she stayed with me through thick and thin and has been my rock!*

*I would also like to dedicate this book to my amazing, supportive, and caring **parents, Valerie Brown and A. Earl Brown Sr**. They have always been my main inspirations in life. Every time I was asked in school to write down who I looked up to, I always AND ONLY put their names down.*

*Last but not least, I want to dedicate this book to my two beautiful, talented, and wonderful **sisters, Rayna Brown and Bianca Campbell**. They have picked me up when I was at my lowest and kept me up when I was at my highest. They have been the perfect sisters that any brother could ask for.*

1
DARK MEMORIES

Running, running
far away.
Escaping memories
of yesterday.

*T*he sound of breaking glass startled Mary awake. The
fourteen-year-old groaned and tugged the blankets away,
silently swinging her feet to the carpet.

"You need to watch your tone with me, Elise!" The raised
voice penetrated the walls. The piercing sound of shattering
glass made its way to Mary's ears again.

"I'm the one who needs to watch my tone?" Elise spat,
"That's rich coming from you. You're the one who made me the
way I am. You know that, don't you?" There was a loaded
silence. Someone opened a door and slammed it shut, leaving
Mary puzzling over her next move in silence.

The door opened again to let out a continued stream of
Elise's yelling, and Mary grimaced. "All you do is blame me
for everything that goes wrong! All you do is act like you're a

saint. I deserve better, Grayson!" Elise's voice had begun to crack from all the yelling by the time little Mary's body slipped out from under her pink covers.

"If this is another one of your nagging sprees, I'm not interested," her father heatedly replied. By now, Mary had settled in front of the door through which the shouting floated, debating what to do.

She peered through the keyhole into the room, holding her breath. There was a carry-on bag on the glorious king-sized bed that she had once loved to jump on, much to her mother's chagrin.

Clothes were strewn everywhere, some haphazardly shoved in the bag, while some barely made it over the top. Right by her mother's vanity, Mary's parents stood in front of each other. The girl could almost smell the hate and anger that permeated the air, like the thick smoke in the kitchen whenever her mom forgot she had something in the oven.

Her body began to ache from crouching at the door. Her heart was thumping like it never had before. Her palms started to sweat. Mary shakily took a deep breath as she watched her parents get into another round of their shouting match.

"You're such an ungrateful woman! You had better take those filthy clothes, put them where they need to be, and stop this nonsense, Elise. I don't have the time for this!"

Elise didn't pay much attention to her husband. She was too busy shoving at his looming figure to get to her carry-on bag. She was leaving. She couldn't deal with the fighting and the emptiness anymore. She was done.

Grayson grabbed his wife by the arm like a petulant child who needed a thorough spanking. He looked her dead in the eye. *"I'm only going to say it once. You get that bag and those clothes back into the closet and go the fu—"*

Mary didn't see the slap, but she heard it, making her clap her hand to her mouth to try and disguise the sharp breath she drew. Loud and clear—**Smack!** The girl watched her parents stare at each other in silence as though they were frozen in time. Her feet really hurt.

"How dare you?" Grayson exclaimed as he grabbed Elise's arm even harder and shook her hard, like one of Mary's raggedy dolls. That was the first time Mary ever saw her mother hit her father. She swallowed, torn between interrupting their latest spat and returning to her room and curling up in bed, buffered by her covers.

Grayson shoved Elise hard at the grand vanity in disgust while muttering the bad words she always cautioned him about when Mary was within range. Elise grunted as she collided headfirst with the vanity and fell in a heap beside it, the mirror shattering all over the dresser.

"When you're done with your pointless whining, you know what to do," Grayson muttered as he flung Elise's clothes onto the maroon rug beside his wife's form on the floor. Elise did not respond.

Silence.

"Get up, Elise. Enough with this; you'll wake Mary." Silence. Mary's heart felt like it might explode from her chest as she repeated her father's words in her mind, *"Get up, get up, please."*

Grayson stopped flinging the clothes. With Elise's favorite green sequined dress in his hands, he stepped tentatively towards Elise as she lay on the rug. *"Elise?"* Elise remained *quiet. In her terror, Mary found her shaking hand reaching for the doorknob automatically.*

Grayson turned her over and gasped sharply as the shimmering green dress fell to the floor. "Elise, wake up!" He swore loudly and grabbed his phone to make a call before hurriedly dropping the phone, gathering the limp Elise in his arms, and rushing to the door where Mary stood wide-eyed and pale as a ghost. The girl hurried away before he turned the knob.

The cold raindrops suddenly pitter-pattering on her face snapped Mary back to the present.

"Ugh," she grimaced. She hated that memory. In fact, she hated every memory her childhood had to offer. Still, that was the one that always came to mind whenever she was in a pickle. Mary chuckled. "I really am in a pickle, aren't I?"

She looked down at her feet. Her nail polish was chipped, she noted numbly. Her feet felt like they were cemented to the ground. She couldn't move.

She wanted to move forward, but a flood of unwanted memories pushed their way to the surface. "Leave me alone," she growled.

There was no one there but her and her thoughts. What good were they anyway? What good was *she* anyway?

Mary closed her eyes and let them stay that way. She couldn't open her eyes. Not when she was about to do what she was about to do. Mary's shivering hands grabbed the rails of the bridge. "How did I get here? How did I get here?" she started chanting like a broken robot.

She took a step away from the railing and clenched her eyes harder. She grimaced again as memories of the previous day pushed to the surface again. This time, harder. This time, she let them.

She opened her eyes to a bleak memory.

"If I were cleverer," Mary thought hazily, "I would be able to tell what time it is now just by observing how far that slant of sunlight has moved around the room." She could see dust motes dance in the ray of sunlight as her eyes felt too heavy to bear. Had she slept? She wasn't sure.

The night faded into the day; thin, watery light came at first, but then the hours passed, and the day seemed to grow surer. Now Mary could sense its solid brightness behind the curtains. But whether sleep had come and gone or had abandoned her altogether was something she couldn't think about clearly. The pale blue drapes were drawn, with a slight gap at the top, and the finger of brightness that had crept around the walls over the last few hours now threatened to touch Mary herself. She didn't want that. God, that was the last thing she needed—a reminder that she was wasting away.

All around the bed lay crumpled clothes, tissues, and books scattered with no care or particular order. Mary was, by nature, quite tidy and put-together. Yet, the room seemed to paint a picture of her mind—her confused and unhappy state—lying in wreckage around her.

How long had she been here for? She couldn't really tell anywhere. Time was a distant construct that her mind failed to comprehend these days. It was hard to accept that the world just went on without her.

If she didn't move at all and just stayed here, maybe it would all just go away.

Her cheeks were wet. The sobbing stopped a while back, leaving only the tears lazily oozing from the corners of her eyes like endless pools of despair and pain. They just came flowing out, and Mary imagined how wonderful it would be if the tears took with them all the pain and agony she felt, leaving her light and free. Free...

Tears were pointless then. They didn't fix anything. Neither did the vodka, but that didn't stop her from guzzling as much of it as she could lay her hands on. For every sip of the drink, her mouth felt horrible—acidic, sore, and dry. Mary decided to test her head, which she strongly suspected would throb the second she tried to move. Cautiously edging off the bed, she groaned like a bear coming out of hibernation. Yep, bad idea.

Oh, how she wanted to curl into a tiny ball on the bed. She didn't want to deal with the state she found herself in. All she wanted was to be lifted like an infant, hugged, cleaned, and laid down again to sleep safe and sound. "Good luck finding anyone that cares enough to do that," she retorted, mocking her own imagination.

Her phone buzzed again. It had been doing that a lot all morning. "I'm so popular," Mary said softly and desperately, managing a bitter, humorless smirk. "You can all wait," she added, her smirk vanishing. She threw her phone, which managed to miss the wall and wobble on the hardwood floor.

Mary walked to the bathroom, stumbling slightly. Turning the light on made her wince, and her eyes and head pounded at the sudden brightness. Leaning forward on the vanity unit, Mary gazed at her reflection. Her dark brown hair was a mess, damp at the temples from crying and sweating, knotted at the ends from grabbing handfuls of her hair in a desperate meltdown the night before.

The night before…

Now, that was a night she never wanted to remember. Her memories had a mind of their own, as she quickly discovered when they came rushing back to her. Screaming, yes, she remembered that much. Most of the screaming and begging was on her part, which made things even more pitiful. She also remembered continuously guzzling the vodka for courage while screaming and weeping at him. She recalled sliding slowly down the wall outside her apartment, unable to make him understand. Unable to make him come back to her.

"Why would he?"

She snapped back to the present as the light flickered off and on. She returned her gaze to her reflection in the mirror. Her pretty face spelled her exhaustion as clear as day, stained with makeup and what could possibly be snot. Her face twisted into a sneer. "Look at you. Just look at yourself. You're disgusting inside and a mess outside. You're a waste of everybody's time."

The emptiness and self-loathing hit harder as she gripped the vanity edge. "You're a waste of space!"

God, why was she so pitiful? She hated being this weak, slobbering mess that couldn't pull herself out of the deep, dark hole. It was like she was high on the absolute craziest narcotics, and she couldn't separate the seamless merging of one time in her life with the next. Everything was happening to her all at once. It was all coming back. God, she needed a drink.

Mary shrieked and grabbed a pot of face cream next to the basin. Gripping it tightly, trembling and desperate, she swung her arm back as though to throw the tub and shatter the glass. Her chest felt empty. "I know this feeling. I've been here before..." Mary gripped the edge of her table even tighter as yet another unwanted memory forced its way through.

Mary recalled it so vividly, as though it were yesterday. Her mind liked to torture her like that. She remembered her stepmother looking slightly bored and irritated by her daughter, who was keen on her attention.

~

It was Mary's fifteenth birthday. She was all alone at home with her father's wife, Miriam.

Mary remembered quietly whispering to her stepmother, "Miriam, *there's no one here yet.* " Of course, there was no one there. Despite the plans and the colorful promises her friends and their parents made, no one would ever dare set foot in the cold, frigid house.

All her childhood friends dreaded her house like a plague, often leaving the poor girl locked up within the four walls of the lavish mansion. Mary begged her stepmother to let her go out. Just this once. She could go to her friend Lauren's house and, at the very least, have a semblance of a normal happy birthday before her father got home.

Miriam felt for the girl. She really did. The house was suffocating enough with the tension that constantly filled it, and she truly would have let the child go and have some fun.

At least one of them deserved to be happy, but Grayson had his own ideas about what was right and wrong for Mary, and it wasn't worth incurring his wrath over. It was better to let him handle it so that peace could reign.

Miriam knew that she had no business making decisions in the household, and Mary knew it too.

Miriam Hart did not want to look at her stepdaughter's face for too long. She didn't want to feel the emotion spilling from those dark depths. Mary spoke again. The party decorations had started to sag, and the food had begun to go stale sitting on the loaded table. The birthday girl pleaded among the reminders for a pardon to leave the house and go to her friends.

The day was quickly passing by, and not one person had shown up to say hello or even wish her a happy birthday. *Miriam paused before she answered coolly, "Ask your father."*

Miriam Hart had long learned that in exchange for her status as "the wife," her seat at all the best luncheons, a beautiful house, and grounds in the best part of town, she let Grayson deal with certain things, and she never disagreed with him on anything. She got the cars, the vacation, the clothes, and the jewelry. In exchange, she gave her husband what he asked for— his word was law in the family. As Grayson set the bar ever higher for his wife and child to win his approval, he became less tolerant of their failure to meet his unbelievable standards by the day.

"Please. You know he'll just say no. I just want to play with one friend, Miriam. I promise I'll be back early. I don't... I don't want to stay here." Miriam's heart broke as she knew all too well what the girl meant by "here."

Miriam eventually gathered the courage to refuse the girl firmly and harshly, saying, "Mary! Stop making a fuss. Ask your father."

At that moment, Grayson Hart walked in, back from work, demanding to know what both ladies were talking about. "Ask me what?"

Grayson Hart's voice was rarely loud. He knew how to use that piercing baritone in a way that carried his words through a room and made everyone turn and give him their attention. An attribute that made him such a great lawyer.

Mary swallowed as she gathered the courage to ask her father to leave their haunted fortress. The man barely skipped a beat as he shut down the request faster than either Miriam or Mary could even blink.

He said Mary had to study. Sitting and giggling about irrelevant things was not going to get her the grades she needed to get the future she needed. "You're staying at home," Grayson said with finality.

Dressed in his beautifully cut Italian suit, Grayson had no idea how much his young daughter wanted to yell at him and call him all the bad names she could think of. The names that tripped off the tongues of the other kids in their class as they dramatically complained about their parents.

"It's my birthday today." The teenager stared defiantly at her father.

"I want to be with my friends. Lauren's house is only down the street, and I promise I'll be good."

"What do you need to go outside for? You have a test on Monday, don't you? You will need to stay home and study. It will not help if you are tired from giggling and gossiping about foolish things. We'll get you a cake if need be." He touched the end of her nose with a light tap. ***"Happy Birthday."***

That day was only one of the many days the young girl felt shattered to her very core. Her father would go on to cause her more pain as time went by.

Mary turned on her heels and left the room without replying, slamming the door hard enough to wake a corpse. It was the only show of defiance she thought she could get away with.

She held back the tears until she was safely in her room. She sunk into her bed and sobbed into the sheets, retreating into her imagination. There, she conjured up the faces that graced her imaginary birthday party. Everyone looked glamorous in their weekend jeans, smiling, huddled around the firelight, giggling, and hugging each other. Oh, it was so much fun.

Mary's chest felt hard and tight, and her hands were clenched into fists, but she felt no anger. It was all gone. All that was left was a deep, black sadness that seemed to swell inside her. The blackness was almost a comfort to her. She had been there many times before. Mary couldn't really define the blackness, but she sometimes thought that if she could just talk to her stepmother, Miriam might have half an idea of what she felt inside. Of course, whether she would admit it was another thing. Miriam was as broken and complicated as they came, and her real mother was... gone.

Mary dragged herself over to the dressing table and stared at herself in the mirror. Her eyes were puffy and red, and her skin was blotchy. "Ugly, stupid girl," she thought. She despised her powerlessness. A wave of bitterness swelled in her chest as she sat there, staring into her own clouded eyes in the mirror.

She wanted to scream. This time, it wasn't for a stupid birthday or loneliness; it was for all the pain that her father had caused. He caused her mother's pain too. Up until the moment he killed her, it was nothing but agonizing pain, and now, he has carried on torturing Mary in her mother's absence. Still, she found herself wanting his approval and affection. She despised how desperately she wanted her father to approve of her, despite what he did. She didn't even know if that was what she wanted. Whether she wanted his love or whether she wanted to purely hate him for what he did to her mother and their family, the girl was conflicted. She knew that much.

That was the last time Mary ever dreamed or spoke of celebrating her birthday. "What use is that?" Her father would say.

~

The alarming strike of thunder in the sky outside jolted Mary back to reality.

Mary opened her mouth to scream in frustration, but she produced no audible sound. It was a trick she had perfected. She screamed profusely at her reflection, hot tears spilling down her face, but the only sound that could be heard was a quiet hiss, like the air escaping through a tiny hole in an overinflated tire.

Stupid, worthless girl. Stupid, worthless girl. Stupid, worthless girl. "Stupid, worthless girl." Mary felt the words tumble right out of her mouth. "Stupid, worthless girl." She said it louder this time, enjoying how the blackness inside seemed to overhaul some of the pain—or was the blackness itself the pain? She could no longer tell. Suddenly, she felt like her teenage self again, sobbing in her bedroom, wishing that something, anything, would change.

Pulling her hair back over one shoulder, she felt a growl of hunger in her stomach. She hadn't eaten since the day before. It didn't matter. Maybe she *was* fat anyway. It's probably why Mark decided to start sleeping with another woman. It was her fault for being ugly, stupid, and fat. "And drunk," Mary added bitterly. She was very drunk.

She staggered out of the bathroom and made her way to the bedside locker, where she grabbed the bottle of vodka. Without pausing, she took a swig. It tasted cold and brimmed like television static would if it had a taste, but it burned in the right way—the way that she needed it to. Now that the bottle was empty, she would have to find a substitute.

Mary had barely touched alcohol before. She certainly didn't get drunk like so many of her college friends regularly did. She didn't see the appeal.

Did the woman he had been sleeping with drink? What was special about her? Was she funny? She must have been smarter than I am. I can only imagine their faces as they laugh hard at me.

Mary shook her head at how pathetic she sounded.

God, she had even thought she might take Mark home to meet her father. She had really thought that they were enough of an item to do that. She was too sure that her father would like Mark. In fact, they could have bonded over how much of a useless mess Mary tended to be. They could tell each other knee-slapping stories about what an idiot she was. She always managed to fall in love with all the wrong people. *"Hey, why not add that to my resume?"* she joked drily. What *did* she know about relationships anyway? Nothing. She knew absolutely nothing.

Then a memory of her and Mark flashed through her mind of a past event that was a symbolic part of their miserable relationship. She shook it off. There was no need to go down that ugly, ugly road.

Mary Julia Pearl Hart stood, returning to her present. She was still there, standing in the cold at the edge of a bridge, ready to give it all up. How on earth did she get to this point?

There was no more hiding in her memories or the past.

This was it.

"This is it. This is it," she chanted.

People do this. People do this. No more pain.

2

PAIN

swimming all alone in a pool of darkness,
it slowly pulls me under...

O h, how far have the mighty fallen?" Mr. Grayson Hart thought to himself as he leaned over the table to grab his lighter. He sat back into his chair and swiveled it around to face the windows of his office, turning his back on the hard lines and the aggressive masculine decoration that the interior designer had felt "defined" him. It was a long way from the truth, he knew—when did he lose those soft edges? The framed family photographs or the spidery child's drawing taped to his monitor? It appeared that with success and notoriety, he had lost every part of himself that he valued.

He lit the lighter and touched his cigar stick to the flame. He puffed and exhaled, watching as the smoky tendrils rose above his head before dissipating into nothing, just like his family had faded. Grayson was well aware that the clock was quickly ticking and that soon it would be time for him to grab his things and leave his office. The building would close for the night, with only the security guards patrolling the corridors like ghosts. It wouldn't do for them to see him, the boss, burrowed away in his office in a miserable and drunken stupor. He would have to go home. Home. He hated the idea of it. It was no longer home, but an empty space that lacked the energy that once filled it. Ghosts and memories floated from its furnishings, mementos of a life that he did not appreciate and subsequently let slip from his fingers.

He exhaled as he continued to stare at the skyline of the city he had come to hate. The city was still very much alive and thriving. He watched from high above as the lights glared from the windows. It was late in the evening, but the city didn't have an off switch. The city had drawn him in with the promise of abundance and success. It had sucked every last ounce of energy from him until he had none left for the things he truly loved. It had dangled the carrot in front of him, and he had chased and caught it, but the city wasn't finished, so to keep that carrot, he had to keep chasing... Keep fighting. The burden grew until it was no longer his family relying on him but his employees and, in turn, their families. His triumph became his burden. He knew it had made him short-tempered and bone-tired; he had become a whole new person. The city was demanding and corrosive. Looking out over the fast-moving lights, he could see it for what it was: a hungry, living, breathing creature. The dense jungle of buildings was constantly expanding, stretching out, and eventually engulfing suburbs with its out-of-control vines, just as it had claimed Gray's life. Only it was eating him from the inside out.

He didn't want to go home and see the face on the walls that continued to haunt him in his sleep and taunt him during the day. He chuckled bitterly as he marveled at how his own home, once a place where he sought refuge and laughed and nurtured his family, was now a place he dreaded worse than death.

Of course, Grayson knew that he wouldn't find his daughter when he got home. Pictures of her graced the walls, a shrine to both her and his wife. He could take them down, but that wouldn't change the situation. A reel of her life played over in his mind. Where did he get it wrong? Was there a pivotal moment, or was it gradual changes over time? When did he become a stranger?

In fact, he couldn't remember the last time he had heard her laugh or seek him out to tell him about her day. When had he become unreachable to his family? He let the cigar smoke envelop him, seeking comfort in the familiarity of the scent. His own father had been unemotional but solid. The cigars he smoked in a nod to his father's memory did not provide him with any peace or reassurance. He had sought to be the family man he craved as a child, but somewhere along the way, his drive to provide had overridden the need to be there. He remembered with a shudder how quickly his wife and daughter would leave the room when he entered with his wired energy, the look on their faces as they searched their minds for a reason to escape—when did they stop being a family? He pondered how long it had been before "the accident." He inhaled and gently pressed and rotated the edge of the cigar against the side of the ashtray, watching the ash crumble and spill into the glass.

Grayson sighed. He imagined how much more Mary would hate him if she learned the truth.

He groaned and rose from his chair, joints creaking and head banging. All the health supplements and gym memberships couldn't hold off old age or time. He swung open his cabinet and picked the first thing that would help him forget the fastest. "Such a mess," he muttered as he distastefully marveled at his newfound, uncharacteristic affinity for alcohol.

He hurried to pour out the liquid into a glass before the memory of his atrocities caught up to him. The amber liquid tumbled into the glass. He marveled bitterly at the expensive bourbon, recognizing the peaty, spiced scent notes that his business associates favored. Too late, he thought as he raised a shaky hand to gulp his regrets. The liquid burned through his chest, settling in his empty stomach like a fiery glow. He sunk back into his buttery-soft executive leather chair and closed his eyes, waiting for glass after glass to take hold of him. It was a roll of the dice as to where the alcohol would take him—to the forgetful oblivion of anesthetized peace or down memory lane, a dangerous journey of torture. Grayson recoiled as he remembered the one night that continued to haunt him, the night that played in his mind on a loop like a bad film, causing his stomach to curdle and his shame and anxiety to rocket.

"You need to watch your tone with me, Elise!" Grayson yelled at his beautiful wife. Elise's lips quivered, and her eyes widened as his finger pointed right in her face. In one swift motion, she swept the glass of wine off the table, sending it crashing to the floor.

"I'm the one who needs to watch my tone? That's rich coming from you. You're the one who made me the way I am. You know that, don't you?" Grayson was quiet. He did know. He hated how filthy he was toward the women he loved.

Elise's face was wet with tears. She turned around and walked into their closet, returning a moment later with clothes in one hand as she slammed the door shut.

18

PAIN

"All you do is blame me for everything that goes wrong! All you do is act like you're a saint. I deserve better, Grayson!" God, the way she called his name, her voice cracking and shaky, tore at him.

He hated that he did what he did and then blamed her for his shortcomings with those horrible words. He wanted to apologize. He wanted to hold his sweetheart in his arms and beg for her forgiveness. Instead, he said, *"If this is another one of your nagging sprees, I'm not interested."*

He wanted to stop staring into Elise's eyes and briefly thought about walking towards their large, king-sized bed, littered with Elise's clothes and her bag, ready to fling her things at her. God, what was wrong with him?

They stood there, frozen in time, beside her vanity table, where she sat every morning and night to put on her creams and lotions. She didn't need them; she was perfect. She always had been.

For a split second, Grayson thought of touching his hand to Elise's arm and making peace. There was no making peace now.

There was no turning back from what he did. He growled at his wife, *"You're such an ungrateful woman! You had better take those filthy clothes, put them where they need to be, and stop this nonsense, Elise. I don't have the time for this!"*

The hypocrisy in Grayson's words choked him as they spilled from his mouth. Elise didn't care for what he had to say as she continued shoving at him, trying to get to their bed with the clothes in her hands. Grayson looked down at her small, resilient figure. He could see the resignation in her stance. She was done with him—with all of it.

Grayson grabbed Elise's arm like he would Mary when she was being bratty in the grocery store. He looked her straight in the eyes. He almost winced at the pain he found in those dark pools brimming with tears.

"I'm only going to say it once. You get that bag and those clothes back into the closet and go to fu— "

He didn't expect the slap. His face stung with pain as he looked at Elise in disbelief. She had never hit him before. He knew he deserved it.

Before he could even caution himself, he flung Elise by her arm, sending her crashing into her vanity. He walked away with the sound of shattering glass behind him.

He reached for the carry-on bag on their bed and threw it on the rug, followed by her other clothes. "When you're done with your pointless whining, you know what to do." He flung some more clothes at his wife's form on the floor.

Elise didn't respond. Great, now he was going to get the silent treatment. The fuming man stood by the large bed as the silence threatened to swallow him.

Grayson stopped flinging the clothes at the rug. He squeezed Elise's favorite green dress in his hands. He bought that dress for her last year and loved seeing her in it. Grayson took a deep breath as he remembered how divine she looked in it. He needed to call off the firearms. He loved this woman too much to see her leave.

"Get up, Elise. Enough with this; you'll wake Mary." That was if the poor girl wasn't awake already. Silence.
He clutched the green dress in his hands as he stepped tentatively towards Elise's form on the floor. He couldn't hear any sobbing. His heartbeat seemed to quicken and slow down at the same time. "Elise?" She didn't respond.

PAIN

Grayson turned her over and gasped sharply as the shimmering green dress fell to the floor. "Elise, wake up!" He cursed loudly and grabbed his cell phone to call 911 and ask for help. After three dials, he cursed again. He couldn't wait. Grayson gathered his wife's body in his arms, tears streaming down his face as he rushed towards the door.

He quickly called Elise's friend, their neighbor Evelyn. Evelyn always had a key to their house, even though Grayson was never comfortable with it. He asked her to fetch Mary while he attended to their "emergency." He didn't care for the annoyance at the early morning call in her voice.

Grayson didn't remember how he got to the car with Elise in the back and made it to the hospital. But when he got there, he didn't need them to tell him. He could feel it in his gut.

That was the second death in the span of three weeks. Grayson didn't remember driving to the bridge, but when the sun rose, he was still there, sitting in his car with his eyes blindly staring at nothing.

First, their unborn son, and now, Elise. His beautiful, beautiful Elise. "I killed them," Grayson said in his empty car.

The sharp shrill coming from Grayson's phone quickly reminded him that he was still in his law office and that it was time to go home. 9:45 pm. He sighed deeply and put out his almost-burnt cigar.

With his jacket, keys, briefcase, and phone in hand, Mr. Hart made his way to the door. He felt like his legs were wading through mud; every step was an effort. As he reached for the doorknob, he hesitated, asking himself if he really wanted to go to his own home; would a hotel give him a restful night's sleep? He doubted it. He squared his shoulders and readied himself to leave. This was his punishment for his behavior—enduring the memories, the looks of disappointment, and the craving to feel his family close and happy again.

He swung the door open either way and walked to the elevator. Soon, he was in his car, driving to the one place in the world that held the most bitterness for him.

He arrived home to a quiet house; the glow of a lamp upstairs reminded him it was not deserted, but he couldn't face going upstairs.

He picked up his things and made his way into his house, heading straight for his home office. He would sleep there tonight, like he did most other nights, surrounded by his paperwork and things he had authority over and could control.

Grayson walked into his office and set his things down. He drew another cigar from the pack and fished out a bottle of brandy with a glass before lazily plopping onto the long couch. Was this it for him now? From one office to another, human contact was just a reminder of his failings.

A spiteful, angry man who darkened and killed everything in his path. He gulped his brandy and sighed.
He hated who he had become. He couldn't even bring himself to think or say Elise's name. It tasted like pain and caustic toxins on his tongue.

Grayson chuckled in the dark room as he puffed twice on his cigar. He hated himself so much. But rather than find a way to heal, he let it poison him. The poison crept into every aspect of his life, including the most important part: Mary.

He picked up his phone and located his daughter's cell phone number in his phone book. He wanted to call Mary and hear her voice—hear her call him "dad." All he was rewarded with was the sound of her cheery voice: "Hey, I can't answer your call right now. Leave a message." He could hear the laughter in her voice at the formality of having to record herself. Was this the only time he would hear her voice again?

Mr. Hart groaned as he turned off his screen and tossed his phone to the other end of the couch. It was his fault that Mary hated him anyway. He couldn't bear to look at her to see what he had done. The devastation he had wreaked on her and the family was irreparable.

All those years, he pushed his daughter away when she probably needed him just as much as he needed her. He just couldn't bear to think of how it would break her heart if she ever found out what he did to her mother. If he thought she hated him now, the hate then would be immeasurable.

He just wished he could make it right. All of it. He took another gulp from his glass. Ah, there were so many things he wanted to change.

Grayson Hart puffed again.

"Oh, how far have the mighty fallen?" He whispered into the cold, dark room.

3
REJECTION

*Rejection, a feeling like cutting
the deepest of our soul
by a razor that causes an affliction.*

His life ended the moment John opened that letter. The pain was not in the message but in the repetition. The relentless assault on his determination had finally won. John felt the paper becoming damp in his grip. The breeze rustled leaves above his head, and slices of sunlight found him and vanished again. This was the most peaceful place he knew: by the disused vestry steps of Our Mother of God Church, out of sight of the road and the passers-by on the pavement, at the back of the church. There was a patch of grass and a few trees, and the peace was only occasionally interrupted by a churchwarden or local dog walker taking a shortcut through the grass to access the road that ran behind Mother of God.

This was where John sat, in the shadow of the church tower, with his knees drawn up to his chest, holding the letter that had finally broken him. Smack in the middle of the night before, John had felt an ache in his heart. There was too much bleakness inside him for him to bear. The letter had broken the last of his resolve. He had left the house, which he shared with his mother, with no money or food. He had thought about turning towards the river to watch the boats haul back and forth and see if watching the heave and sway of the water would bring some calmness to his troubled mind. However, he was drawn back here, as he had been before. He had laid down on the ground, drowning in the darkness, feeling only the tickle of the grass under his body and the breeze that disturbed the trees, certain that he wouldn't be missed.

Why did he choose this place? Were his religious beliefs playing into his subconscious? Was it because some part of him believed that God loved him and was watching over him more closely here? Maybe he hadn't caught God's attention enough at home in his narrow bedroom, working away and trying to keep from being under everybody's feet.

Maybe he would feel the comfort and love that religious folk talked about here. He believed in God and prayed often enough, but perhaps he would be heard better here, near God's sanctuary.

John barely missed a Sabbath day in church when he was younger, back when his mother had time for that sort of thing. He had even harbored an ambition to join the church choir, but his brothers soon teased him out of that thought. He remembered clearly the taunts about how he would "wear a dress to sing like an angel." But John still loved the idea of standing in the wooden pews with the scent of beeswax polish drifting over him, being one of the people who were trusted to have responsibilities during church services. He liked the idea of belonging to something bigger than himself, somewhere he

25

might gain a little respect. The songs also caught his fancy. Not songs per se. The hymns were sung in the highest soprano. But that made them sound less beautiful than they were. The soaring church organ and the voices lifted up together in the Sunday morning service were among John's favorite memories.

John also hoped that some of the kids in the choir might become his friends. He barely had any friends at school, but maybe the kids would give him a chance he never seemed to get in school.

One Sunday, when he was eight years old, he hadn't eaten enough breakfast and was being hurried out of the door by his mother, all done up in her Sunday-best-for-church outfit. Halfway through the church service, he felt gray inside, drifting somewhere behind his own closed eyes. When Father Matthew strode past him with the incense, something overwhelmed him, and he fainted—right there in the pew, next to his mother and wide-eyed brothers.

When John came to, he was lying on a wooden table in the vestry, with Father's kind eyes fixed on him. "Ah, he's back with us!" he exclaimed, putting on a smile of relief, helping John to a sitting position. John took in the rows of richly colored choir robes, the priest's paraphernalia, and the warmly lit room. Father Matthew had brought out a barrel of sugared biscuits and given two to John. A few boys from the choir had gathered around and helped the priest, all while this occurred in front of the entire church, with many onlookers concerned and curious. Did he just interrupt an entire church service with his little episode? With so many watching in shock and worry, there was a sense of confusion. To this day, the event has stuck with him for whatever reason.

REJECTION

It struck John how peaceful this busy little scene was. There was this air of kindness and calm that John very much wanted to be part of. He almost asked there and then if he could stay. He looked at the surplices hanging from the wooden hooks. One would fit him well, he was sure. Then he could be a trusted friend of this welcoming group and find his place where people would see him singing on a Sunday morning and tell his mother what a fine boy he was.

Would things have turned out differently? Would he still be here now, desperate and alone, outside? How many people is he failing right now? Had he come back here because that unassuming moment in his life was the last time he experienced some happiness? Maybe if he thought about it long enough, he would see that, in his eighth year, he still expected to be happy. After that, things didn't seem so bright. And now, as he tried to make his way in the world and tried so hard to earn a place at a college so he could finally make his mother proud of him, things had never seemed bleaker. But an influential motive for him was that maybe, just maybe, he could have a fresh start. This was his opportunity to put all the despair and negative life events in the past, an opportunity to be reformed into a completely different person. That person he really wanted to be, that he had always dreamed of being, had countless daydreams just staring at the wall, encompassed by his usual loneliness. And why couldn't he? He would go to his dream school, where no one knew him, and take the campus by storm. He took a moment to fantasize about it.

John shut his eyes and imagined a world where he had his own dorm room with banners from his clubs decorating the walls and a family who celebrated him and hugged him as he delivered the wonderful news. What a great feeling that would be! Maybe they'd all go out for pizza that night to celebrate, and he'd ride shotgun because he was the man of the hour.

He'd order his favorite Four Seasons with extra cheese and accept a root beer from his brother. They'd laugh together, share their dreams for the future, and see their mother's face glowing with soft happiness at her children's happiness—an exciting world out of reality.

John opened his eyes before the daydream could continue. He was not ordering pizza. No one was cheering for him. He was sitting alone under a tree, with nothing in the world but a letter saying that yet another university had rejected him.

Murphy University was his dream school. He visualized the beautiful campus with Victorian-style buildings, state-of-the-art classrooms with the latest technology, and courses taught by the most highly regarded professors. Mostly, he thought of the opportunities that come with it. Opportunities for future happiness, where he would be the "master of his fate." He remembered one of his favorite and most influential poems, "Invictus" by Rudyard Kipling. This poem, which he loved so much and so passionately, articulated through its words how man is always in control and the "master of our fates and captain of our souls," regardless of how many times we have been beaten down and even in our roughest of times. Murphy University would be that path, that opening, that would allow him to conquer his fate and his future.

Recently, he'd been turned down by two other top colleges despite his perfect grades. Even with that, he had hope. But this letter from Murphy University had driven him here. He had dared to believe. He had ripped open the envelope with a pounding heart, letting his hopes run away with him. It was daring to think that this might be the gateway to the rest of his life.

Those words, *"We are sorry to inform you that your application has been unsuccessful. If you would like further..."* John went no further. No matter how hard he worked or how much better his grades were than any other candidate's, a shadow fell across everything he did, and the universities knew it somehow. Is it possible they could sense that this lonely and desperate boy was not one of them? That, with his imperfect looks, he would stand out too harshly against the sea of good-looking, confident, and worthy students? Did the shadows that had grown within him over the years somehow reveal themselves in a way that he couldn't imagine? His thoughts wandered far and wide. His sense of rejection found a home.

Where did he fit in? He didn't even fit into his own family. His brothers, Jake and Sean, were both tall and handsome, with well-chiseled bodies that would make Adonis weep. They could hold their ground anywhere and have shrugged off their poor start, with their dad leaving home and their mother working every hour to keep a roof over their heads. Jake, his eldest brother, had progressed to a junior management position in an insurance company. He'd gone from an entry-level position with a job administering to the front office of the insurance company to, only five years later, living in a detached house in another state with his own family and an executive position.

Jake had already settled down with the girl of his dreams, Monica, and no one doubted that Jake and Monica were in it for the long haul. They complimented each other perfectly and shared a steely competitive streak that saw them constantly aiming for the next stage, the next reward, and the next realized ambition of their lives. They called each other "soulmates."

Jake had more than his fair share of charm, which partly came from genuinely enjoying talking to and being around other people—particularly if they happened to be pretty women. He never failed to keep them smiling from ear to ear as he sweet-talked them, with his cuteness dripping all over. Jake's charm, though, seemed to vanish when dealing with his youngest brother, and John had to put up with thinly disguised jibes about his appearance, height, and any other shortcoming he could be bothered to think of.

Sean was only five years older than John, but it might as well have been thirty. Sean had interned with a local construction firm and somehow was retained to assist the marketing manager there. Within two years, Sean had secured himself a niche as a marketing expert for the construction firm. He was a single, fine man with a company car, decent suits to wear every day, and a cell phone that never seemed to stop ringing.

John's older brothers had been a team before he was born, maybe because they were closer in age. They were perfect allies in teasing his esteem out of him. John often spotted his mother sighing and shaking her head as he hesitantly walked past her at home. Many times, he overheard her lamenting about how John had not been the girl she wanted. John's ears caught his mother telling people that his brothers teased him because two boys were enough for any family. Clueless and with no deviant intentions, she added that if John had come as a girl instead, her big brothers would have treasured her, and life could have been much more perfect for all of them. He had always heard and absorbed that unwanted feeling. The boy soaked and reveled in the harsh reality of not being wanted or desired by anyone anywhere. From a young age, John had been made to feel like he was a misfit, an awkward boy who didn't endear himself to anyone.

When their father finally left after years of bitterness and unhappiness on the parts of both his parents, John wept bitterly. He didn't cry for his mother, as he didn't understand how hard her life would get as a single parent to three young boys. Nor did he cry for the loss of his father, as Ronnie had been a stranger to regular employment, liked to wager too many bets with other people's money, and was all-around just about as far from the perfect father as it was possible to be. No, John cried because he felt responsible. If he had been a girl, then his dad would have thought his third-born to be a perfect angel, and that mythical, laughing, lovely little girl would have been a strong bond to the family.

The diminished family had limped along, with Christmases, summers, and birthdays passing by, until it was time for John to decide what he wanted for his life. His mother had persuaded Jake to offer John a small job working at his office, but John declined. His ambitions were well beyond working in an office with his brother, who wouldn't appreciate his efforts. Psychology penetrated his ambitions and interests and was something he deeply wanted to explore. He also had this little aspiration of publishing a book about himself sometime in the future. Despite his demoralizing existence and the heavy feelings and emotions that came with it, he wanted to be one of those successful counselors who helped young and dispirited kids like himself. He didn't want other kids to grow up with heavy hearts and sad days like he did.

One thing that John could hold his head up about was his intellect. There was little doubt that his intelligence surpassed that of his peers and his brothers combined. His brain assimilated information easily and processed it quickly with the utmost brilliance. He had a strong sense of right and wrong and what it meant to be the underdog. It was the underdog he wanted to fight for. He had no interest in living a flashy lifestyle or helping those who did. All he wanted was to uplift those who were just like him and bring joy and happiness into their lives. If he wasn't going to have any of those, then at least others should.

John pushed himself harder than any parent or teacher could have. He had a goal he set out to achieve. He wasn't interested in the trappings of being some wealthy professional; although it would be nice to have his own place, furnished to his taste, and a haven from the world, he hungered for the good he could do in the world.

And now, from those lofty dreams, from those long nights of revising and studying, comes this tragedy: a desolate, searing isolation that couldn't be shaken. The rejections had trampled on his ambitions. John had been buoyant enough to apply again to other universities, but now, this letter came along with the creeping realization that he was not going to make it, that his family had been right all along, or at least what they had always thought of him: a misfit and a loser. A loser at life and at everything. He couldn't even inspire his own family to value him; how could he persuade the world?

John rubbed his eyes with his fingertips. All the effort, all the work, had been for nothing. After all the years of being teased, having no friends, being taunted by his brothers, and being ignored by his mother, he had enough. *"I've had enough of it all,"* John thought bitterly.

Just then, one of the infrequent visitors to this quiet place passed by and called out a greeting. The church staff member was a jolly-faced man in his sixties, wearing a crochet sweater and the kind of hat that fishermen wear in children's books.

"How are you doing there, son? Are you okay? I've seen that you've been out here for a while now, and I thought I'd better check that you're alright." The older man slowly crouched to meet John's gaze with his older, wiser eyes.

John looked at his watch. It was now late afternoon; the world was starting to dim, and he had been sitting in this single spot for hours after waking up from sleeping on these same grounds the night before. The man's kindness was almost as much as John could bear. It threw his own desolation into relief, like trees lit by sunlight yet framed by a dark, thunderous sky.

Tears started to slowly well up in John's eyes as he felt a rush of emotion fill his heart. He wanted to voice out his pain. He wanted to take the man's hand and accept the kindness offered, but it was too late for that. It was all far too late.

Grabbing his thin coat from the grass, John had no choice but to manage the vaguest nod to the kindly man and leave this place of prayer and reflection. It had been the last place, which might have comforted him, but John walked away in utter despair. As John abruptly yet kindly walked off, the man looked at him walking away, sensing the deep sorrow in the young boy, and hoped that God would intervene.

Distant rolls of far-off thunder began to roar in the clouds, drumming through the air like an oncoming giant. The air felt electric. That atmosphere before a storm broke—as though everything was being held back until suddenly, all the elements would unleash their worst—John felt that keenly, as though the storm was about to break inside him as well.

As he walked away, John knew deep in his heart that what was truly gnawing at him on the inside was not the content of that letter or the ones before it. It was the significance they held. He was a filthy, undesirable reject that no one would ever want anywhere. The truth cut him deep like a surgical blade as he continued to walk.

The dark purple pre-storm sky lashed with ribbons of black seemed to seep into his very being as he walked away. The darkness around him became part of him, and John buried his head down into his collar, shutting out the busy world around him. He felt overwhelmed and horrified by the thoughts in his head, yet certain he knew what to do next.

4
ESCAPE ROUTE

Cruel and relentless
No matter what, there is never a true escape...

E leanor took a deep breath as she cleared the debris from the table she was waiting at the diner. With the two messy trays in hand, she made her way to the frantic kitchen, past the sweating cooks, and over to where she would dump them for Lana to clean up.

At 51, the mother of three was very well aware that this was hardly a job fitting for her age. The hard tiled floors were tough on her feet, the sporadic lighting caused her to squint through her glasses at her order pad, and the hours she spent pacing from the heat of the kitchen to the demands of the hungry customers caused her body to ache. She returned out front to the group of rowdy teenagers that had just stormed into the diner.

"Can I take your order?" Eleanor asked in a friendly tone, notepad and pen in hand. Quickly comporting themselves upon seeing their elderly waitress, the teenagers called out their orders as Eleanor's pen glided automatically across her notepad.

She approached the bright counter, yelling the order to Mikey, who then yelled the order to Paige. When Eleanor glanced at the dining area, there were two newly occupied tables: a couple at one of the tables by the door and her youngest son at the table farthest away from the others, ensconced in a dark corner.

Eleanor took a deep breath at the sight of her boy in the gloom. With his hoodie-clad figure shrouded from sight and his head down, it was almost easy to miss John or completely ignore that he was there. Eleanor sighed. That's what she'd been doing for nearly his entire life. Miss him or completely ignore him. Not unlike his brothers but unfortunate, John was different. They had blossomed into striking young men, but John's looks and comparing himself to them had held him back. While they sought the limelight and used their good looks to their advantage, John was unaware of his other most important attributes: his kindness and huge heart. He seemed to shrink into the background and shy away from praise. He had grown into an attentive and thoughtful young man. She saw herself reflected in him when he smiled, her dark hair framing his face, and the dimples that marked her cheeks were almost identical to her youngest son's. He had been an easy baby, happy to observe quietly. Then he quickly grew into an easy-going child; he would find joy in the smallest things, appreciating details around him that others easily missed in day-to-day life. Eleanor waited for his teenage years to bring her testing times; surely, there would come a time when he tested her, just as his brothers had done before him. However, John seemed older, way beyond his years, working hard to better himself and use his exceptional intelligence to exceed anyone's expectations. But even with these achievements, he never celebrated or bragged. Often, she would not learn of the grades or awards until she came across a certificate or letter stashed away out of sight. Where his older brothers shone and celebrated, John faded. The comparisons of his looks to those of his brothers held him back, and as he physically couldn't compete, he forgot the many other things that made him exceptional.

How she hated that it had to be that way! Eleanor headed over to the giggling couple to take their orders. The dimpled 20-something-year-old giggled at her partner again as she struggled to decide what she wanted to eat. Eleanor stood patiently, waiting for her customer to decide.

When the giggling and indecision were over, the couple settled for what they wanted, much to Eleanor's relief. She headed to the counter for the ordering-yelling-chain routine. With her back to the dining area, Eleanor silently prayed that more people would come in so she wouldn't have to face her son.

When she turned back, the same people were still sitting in the diner. The giggling couple, the rowdy teenagers, the college student fiercely ruling on her computer while chugging her black coffee, and the two girls who seemed more interested in their phones than in talking to each other.

Deep sigh.

Eleanor traced her steps carefully to the dark corner where her son sat. She saw him tense up the moment her seat squeaked with her weight. The mother and son were quiet for a while as they settled into the awkwardness.

"They said no," John began.

Eleanor let out a breath she didn't know she had been holding. She watched her son's bottom lip quiver as though he was about to let out a dam of tears.

This was the fourth? Fifth rejection? Eleanor couldn't remember anymore, but she just knew that the more rejection letters that came in through the mail, the more John would sink into depression. She wanted to reach out to him and be there for him. She didn't think she even knew how. She hated how she felt like a stranger to her own son.

As she watched John's shoulders rise and fall as he bowed his head in pain, the 51-year-old realized that these letters were significant to both of them but for completely different reasons.

Eleanor knew one thing was constant about whatever she and John were hoping for in those letters. Escape. But for different reasons.

Being the mother of three grown men had taught her one thing, if nothing else. She knew how to read her boys like the back of her hand. Her John, the poor thing, was seeking escape, a refuge from whatever it was that haunted him in their home. Nonetheless, she knew she played a big part in his search for escape. The boy had always been exceptionally smart, so there was no other place he could seek refuge besides his books and school.

Eleanor's search for escape was much different. She sought to be rid of the guilt she felt. For some reason, she couldn't shake off the guilt that washed over her every time she looked at her John. Those gorgeous, vibrant brown eyes seemed to touch the deepest parts of her soul, reminding her how much she had failed to love him enough. From a young age, it seemed that he tried to shrink himself as though he hoped people wouldn't see him and poke fun at him. That never really worked with the bullies, but that was a trait that followed him into his later years. She blamed herself for not protecting him and for contributing to what he needed protection from.

Eleanor wanted the shrinking, quivering boy to look at her and find solace. She wished John could see the words she was struggling to say. The woman didn't hate her son. No, on the contrary, she had a deep, unparalleled love for her boy. But, for some reason, she held back from loving him as a mother should openly love her son.

It was hard for Eleanor. Seeing him everywhere reminded her of what she had lost all those years ago, of what she could have had if things had gone the way she wanted—the way she needed them to. The diner door chimed, heralding the arrival of people looking to fill their bellies. Eleanor sighed and leaned across the table to gently touch John's shoulder.

"I'm so sorry, John. There will always be another," she calmly said. Frozen in the awkward interaction and her attempt at consoling her son, Eleanor hoped that her words would come to pass. She hated to see her son so sad. She hated not being able to do anything about it either.

She got up from the table, muttering that she would see him at home, briefly hesitating before telling him she loved him while fishing out her notepad and pen. She tromped to the table where the three new customers sat patiently waiting for someone to take their orders.

She didn't notice when John slinked out of the diner and off to God knew where. But when she did notice his absence, she quickly became sad. Even though they seldom spoke, the boy's presence had always been calming. She remembered all the nights she lay in bed sobbing, and his small frame would slip into her bed and hug her tightly. Eleanor sighed again.

Soon, her shift would be over, and she would be off to her next job.

By the time Eleanor was done with her shift, it was almost 7 p.m., and the sky was dark and threatening to pour. She picked up her feet as she briskly walked to her rickety car to make her way to her destination. There, she would meet two vibrant girls named Irene and Gianna-Louise. Irene and Gianna-Louise were far from girls when one looked at them, but the 84-year-old twin sisters were as colorful and youthful as they could be. The twin sisters lit up when they were referred to as "the girls" or "the ladies." Eleanor could understand why. Time stole a lot from people.

Being a home health aide was not as terrible as anyone would expect it to be. In fact, Eleanor found herself enjoying her job sometimes. Being loved, appreciated, and wanted by these people made her feel less depressed about her life and where it was headed. Of course, they had no choice but to need her to be there for them, but it still gave her hope that she could make some things right for some people. Her own family was nowhere near perfect, but she could do something for these people, and that would have to be enough.

Irene and Gianna-Louise, who insisted on being called Lou, were the two elderly women Eleanor catered to on weekdays after her shift at the diner and on her off days till Irene's daughter, Caroline, and her husband, Keith, came back home. Caroline and Keith were two well-to-do, high-profile art dealers living in the finer parts of the city. Irene, Caroline's mother, had battled cancer for many years. After several rounds of chemo and the treatments every expensive clinic had to offer, recuperation was a little more delicate than usual. After failed attempts at keeping her in the best nursing homes, Caroline and

Keith brought her to their home to live with them, and Eleanor was only one of her many caretakers. Irene never went anywhere without her twin sister, Gianna-Louise, and vice versa. At 84, both women were as inseparable as two young twin sisters who did everything together and wore matching outfits.

The elderly women were firecrackers in their different ways. Irene had recently suffered a stroke and was only starting to regain basic motor skills, including speaking. Even with that, anyone could see that the woman had a golden soul that lived life. Anyone could see that she was happy. Eleanor wanted to be happy too.

But with the life she was given, there was no telling what would become of her at that age or even in the next year. The smile on her face quickly dropped. She was back to her own reality.

Eleanor's thoughts occupied her as she slowly drove to the gated neighborhood where Caroline and Keith Waters resided with their elderly companions. By the time she was let into the estate and past the Waters' domineering gates into the luxurious mansion, Irene and Lou were seated in the living room listening to Peggy Lee. Irene was in her wheelchair, and her twin, Lou, was on the couch with her walker beside her. The warm smile on Lou's face and the bright, recognizable flicker in Irene's eyes enveloped Eleanor as she dropped her bags and greeted them happily.

"Oh, Ellie, dear, you must see what I made just yesterday," Lou began without missing a beat. Lou loved to knit and made the most fabulous pieces. Of course, there were only so many mug holders and blankets that she could force Eleanor to take home, but she did try.

The silver-haired knitter offered a half-done sweater to Eleanor with a shaky, weathered hand. It was a precious purple sweater in the making, and judging from the size, it was for Caroline and Keith's daughter, Paige. "The kids are coming back soon?" Eleanor asked as she returned the sweater to Lou, telling her how gorgeous it was.

Irene replied slowly, "Yes, yes. In... In a few days." "Very good, Irene!" Eleanor cheered as the elderly woman completed her sentence with little difficulty. As Eleanor listened to Lou finish gushing about her grandchildren's homecoming after so many weeks, she rolled Irene's wheelchair out of the grand living room to the slope by the staircase, leading her upstairs, where she would wash up in the bathroom. Lou continued knitting, humming softly to the Peggy Lee classic emanating from the speaker on the glass centerpiece.

As Eleanor got set to clean up Irene and get things done, she retreated to her earlier thoughts. She could remember those days when she was pregnant with her third child. There was a skip in her step, a certain glow about her, and a sweet twang to her voice. She didn't need anyone to tell her because she could see it herself.

She could feel it too. Every time her baby kicked, she would touch her hand tenderly to her growing belly and smile. "My baby girl," she would softly say.

Of course, when the baby came, it wasn't a girl. It was her John. Her John, with his beautiful brown eyes and his head full of hair. Her marriage was almost dead before her pregnancy, but after they found out they were expecting, it was suddenly like the clouds let up over their dying love, and they couldn't wait to meet the little one— sometimes, they would refer to the child as their little princess. They didn't know for certain, but they hoped.

When John came, his father found yet another excuse to boycott caring for the family, and Eleanor knew it was just her and her sons from then on. The mother of three often chided herself for thinking a child—boy or girl—could save her marriage. As ridiculous as it sounded, she truly believed there was still a chance with the shameless man.

Her so-called husband would be gone for hours and hours, and then he would return home empty-handed, having gambled away all the money he had gathered in the past couple of days. It didn't take long for those long hours he spent outside to turn into days at a stretch. Eleanor seldom saw her husband; when she did, he barely even looked at her. The constant fighting and arguing eventually graduated into a never-ending silent treatment. She had known him for almost all her life. She had married him almost straight out of high school. It was suddenly like he didn't know her anymore and she, him.

As she carefully helped Irene out of the bathroom and into her shared bedroom with Lou, Eleanor continued to marvel at her stupidity for thinking anything could have saved her marriage—and her life.

Eleanor continued her work absent-mindedly as she got the older woman dressed and settled her in her wheelchair while she changed the bedding before getting her ready to eat.

So many years later, Eleanor's suffering and pain still hadn't waned. The little boy who came at a time when everything seemed to be going so wrong in her life became the one she cherished the most. She remembered when he would wait up for her till midnight when she came home tired from work, sometimes with a glass of water, other times with a smile just for her.

She kept those memories jealously tucked in the deepest recesses of her heart. Sometimes, she wondered if John remembered those days before the gnawing distance between them grew.

She wouldn't blame him if all he remembered was the awkwardness and silence. As the child with the twinkling eyes grew older and got more battered by the world around him, so did Eleanor. She sank further into the decay that was her life. By then, her husband was long gone, but his debts and the darkness he left behind remained.

As her boys grew, Eleanor watched herself crumble under the weight of it all. It didn't help that she had no one to turn to. Decades ago, she held an infant John in her arms as she cried helplessly, looking to the heavens for help, a sign, or anything.

Despair gripped Eleanor. There was nothing then, and there is nothing now. And tomorrow and the days after, there would probably still be nothing.

5
EXPECTATIONS

Expect rain but
the sun shines brightly
Expect Sunlight but
Rain covers you fully

Mary stared at herself in the mirror as if a light of recognition might go off if she looked hard enough. Mary felt like she had a smaller personality screaming inside her, and that small version diminished by the minute. It seemed to shrink back behind her eyes until all she saw were pools of watery green and the shell outside.

The words to a song she had loved as a child floated into her consciousness, and she began humming the tune, even though she knew that no one was listening.

Mary loathed the small creature bound to weakness inside her. It seemed to be caught in webs set by her father's ambitions for her, by everyone's expectations of her, by the accumulation of her past destructive relationships, and most importantly, by the weight of her mother's death. No matter how that part of her struggled, she was stuck in a web of what she was supposed to be rather than the person she really was or wanted to be.

The sudden rage erupted. "I hate you!" She spat the words at her reflection in the mirror. She felt more venom build in her throat and yelled again, "I hate you! I hate you!" Fresh tears coursed down her face, and she felt the fine mask of salt from her last tears softening and cracking to accommodate the new ones.

Mary could see the girl she was way before she started her long and demanding studies at one of the finest law schools in the country. It all came back to her as vividly as if the scene had occurred yesterday. She was so buttoned down and meek. Her father had called her into his study on the eve of her departure for law school and shown her a photograph of himself when he was her age. The Grayson Hart in the picture was strong-jawed, slim, and sporty-looking. He still had that rakish twinkle in his eyes that managed to make him look good-natured and serious-minded at the same time.

Mary knew that her paternal grandfather had been blue-collar through and through and that Grayson had been the first in his family to receive such high academic success. He clawed his way to the top in a traditionally lower-middle-class world. Grayson had opened his own doors into a world of respect, wealth, and hard work, and he wasn't going to have Mary fail to follow in his footsteps. She was a product of his strict and unwavering ambitions and perspective and, as he strongly felt, an ultimate representation to others of who he was.

"When I was your age, Mary, I didn't party. I didn't drink. I didn't fool around with a string of girls. I wouldn't deny that I sometimes had the urge to get involved in such activities, but when I think of my father and his failure to be the boss through wealth and influence, I get my head in place. He had to follow orders at all times. He had to always clock in and out at specific times. If he needed two hours off to see his son on his birthday or to spend time with his sister, who was gravely ill with very little time left in this world and God knows what else, he had to ask for permission, and I would rather chew on broken glass than live such a life. That was not freedom. That was bondage with invisible shackles."

"I wanted to work hard enough to ensure I never had to ask for permission to do anything and was always in the financial situation to do everything I desired. I wanted to be the man giving permission. The only way to be the best lawyer in the best firm with the biggest cases was to work harder and longer than anyone else. And I sacrificed all those things to do that and be where I am today—where I not only want you to be but where I expect you to be someday."

Grayson had turned his leather chair toward the window and stood. He was almost silhouetted against the bright office window, and behind him, in the garden, Mary could see the perfectly manicured lawn and flower beds.

"I have certain expectations for you, so you are not allowed to let this family down, Mary. You carry this family name, and you mustn't drag it through the mud. History counts for everything. I expect you to be the best. I expect you to want to be the best. The world is awaiting those who plow a forward furrow, Mary. Keep your eyes on the prizes that await you. I have done everything possible to give you the best chances in life. Now, it is up to you. From this moment on, it is your responsibility to be the best. Second best is never good enough."

Grayson Hart slowly turned around to face Mary, his gaze fixed on hers as if peering deep into her soul. The sunlight made his slightly gray hair look somewhat metallic, and his eyes were piercing. Mary seemed to shrink under his gaze and recoil within herself. "Second best is not good enough, Mary," her father said flatly, dismissing any argument or complaint. To him, this was fact and non-negotiable.

Mary quickly came back to reality—this dreadful one. And now, on this desperate day, "I can't always be the best, Dad." Mary's voice was a plaintive moan. "I'm not the best. Never will be."

And yet, hadn't Mary consistently been the most studious and accomplished student among her peers, in every school she had ever attended, even in grade school? Mary had excelled year after year, all the way through college, where she was elected valedictorian of her class and gave the student commencement speech.

Hadn't she been awarded not only many prestigious academic awards and been offered several law scholarships but also been dubbed the most promising student by her professors? And didn't she garner compliments on her beauty wherever she went? Mary knew that people thought she was pretty. She thought back to how she was even seen as special by an ex-boyfriend whom she dared not reminisce about. She shuddered. Her romantic back catalog was distressing to even think about.

Mary seemed only to be attracted to boys or men who would initially charm her, then ultimately reinforce all the hateful things she thought about herself. She had a couple of friends with whom she was close enough to talk about her inability to find a decent guy. Charlotte, one of her friends, pointed out bluntly that Mary wasn't interested in anyone being nice to her, almost as though she knew its authenticity. Mary was only prepared to believe negative things about herself and allowed her ex-boyfriends—plural in high numbers—to bully her and take her fragile self-esteem down a few more notches. Then, they would emotionally abuse her until they got bored and dumped her. It was like clockwork.

Mary winced at the thought of Charlotte. What a good, honest friend Charlotte had been. Their friendship had been icy ever since they had the boyfriend conversation. Charlotte had suggested that Mary only fell for boys who treated her like her father did. Grayson wanted his daughter to be the best but constantly stripped away her self-worth. She knew that Charlotte had been right, but she didn't want to hear it.

Suddenly, Mary snapped her head back and turned away from her reflection. Pausing momentarily to pull on an oversized shirt, she stumbled downstairs. Her housemates, Jen and Beth, were both away for the weekend, Jen back home at her parents' house upstate, and Beth with the new hot guy she had hooked up with recently.

Mary went through the tiny sitting room to the kitchen. Ignoring the note left on the table for her, she swung the doors of the cupboard open. "Ah-ha." A playfully bitter note crept into Mary's voice. "Look what Beth has left for me." Mary grabbed the bottle of rum, which Beth had stashed from a previous wild night of hers.

Given her housemate's love for wild partying and rabid drinking, Mary was amazed it was still there.

Mary opened the bottle with brutal force and poured a shot into an egg cup. "Cheers, Dad," she winced as the fiery liquid went down. She started to retch slightly but swallowed hard and got herself under control again. Balling her fist on the table, she poured another large shot of alcohol, followed by a smirk. "Down the hatch."

Mary imitated her stepmother's favorite little cocktail hour witticism, something she picked up from one of her friends from England, the wife of a colleague at the law firm. It burned less this time but was still unpleasant. But somehow, unpleasant became pleasant now.

Mary didn't want to dwell on that, so another shot was tipped out of the bottle into her cup.

"Ah, now that's better." The rum was rubbing away the edges nicely. All of those hideous thoughts and the hatred for herself remained, but with the alcohol came a kind of acceptance, a strange calm. She took another shot, and as it came down, so did the darkness of every bad thought she had about herself. As she consumed more drinks, every negative thought consumed her; she had tried to be perfect for everyone and failed. She not only failed but also messed up, screwed up, and now she was just messed up. A tiny voice somewhere was trying to shout to her that she had done well and that she had a place at this prestigious school. She should be proud of herself.

And how about being pretty? The little voice reminded her that every other person saw a pretty, smart woman well on her way to a wonderful life and career.

"Oh, shut up," Mary slurred, "I'm not anything. I'm nothing but a failure. If they're all too dumb to see that, then so what?" She wanted so badly to make every fiber of her being believe it.

The final shot of rum blurred the lines even more, and she fell into complete darkness. Look at how her ex-boyfriends treated her. They couldn't all be wrong, could they? There was a reason everyone treated her like a piece of trash. What was that saying? Her mind, buzzing with alcohol, searched for the phrase that kept leaping out of comprehension. Something about rubbish. "Throwing out the rubbish?"

Ah yes. That's it: "Good riddance to bad rubbish."

"Good riddance to bad rubbish," Mary said the words aloud, and they echoed slightly through the kitchen. That's what they'll say. If... if I... wasn't here anymore, that's what they'd say.

"No, no," cried the tiny voice, "They love you. They value you. Your friends care, and your father cares." But that tiny voice was diminishing by the second. She could hardly hear it anymore. She tried to push the darkness out, but it stayed.

And it was lying anyway. Or was it? What is real now? Was the rum helping her see things clearly, or was it confusing her? The rum was poisoning her mind.

"Would they cry?" Mary closed her eyes. She couldn't imagine her father crying. She had never seen him cry. She found it far easier to imagine his anger at having a daughter who was the ultimate failure. "Good riddance," he'd probably think, "Good riddance to bad rubbish." There was worse to come anyway. Mary didn't know, but a snake was coming to bite her on the heel of her foot, and not even her holy house of self-loathing could save her. It was coming for her, fast.

6

BROKEN

The soul is a dark barren field
In the cold rain;
The soul is a broken field
Ploughed by pain.

John left the churchyard, feeling the eyes of the kind church staff member upon his retreating figure.

He walked briskly with his head down and his hands buried in his pockets. Uncertain of his destination, John cast a shifty glance around. He saw laughing moms happily pushing along strollers and little children skipping while enjoying the bright day; people in formal wear carrying take-out coffees; and older people arm in arm, strolling and gazing into windows. Everyone seemed to have a place—everyone but him. Did he stand out? Was it possible to tell just by looking at him that he didn't fit in?

Suddenly, emotions came rushing over John, and the desire to talk with someone gripped him. Anyone. He needed to connect with someone and sensed somehow that it was important that he act on this impulse. John felt as though key moments or choices were lining up before him and that picking one became a necessity. With this in mind, he wanted very much to follow the compulsion to speak with his mother or even one of his brothers. He'd even speak with his father if he had any clue about his whereabouts.

John took the phone from his pocket and gripped it tightly. His hand shook as he found his mother's number and dialed it. His heart jumped at each ring, dread gripping his soul. As if confirming his fears, he was sent straight to voicemail. John lowered the phone and looked at it with a weakened glare. *"What did I expect? My own mother despises me."*

Chance is gone. And now comes the creeping realization that if he had made the call, he would have made the wrong decision. If he tried to speak with his mother, she would be too busy to listen to him. Jake and Sean would be wholly incapable of understanding why the rejection from Murphy College was so devastating. They'd shrug and tell him to apply elsewhere or just "go get a job, bro." That's how things happened in their world. They wouldn't be able to comprehend that the letter felt like an axe was planted in his back and then gruesomely twisted to set the pain in, pushing him towards a fate that was as inevitable as it was undesirable. Hadn't he been pushed down this path for years? The rejection from Murphy University was the catalyst for his despair now, but he had battled disappointment after disappointment for so long. His sadness and sense of failure had followed him for so long that he could barely remember life without them.

John had never felt like a success at anything. No, that was not a feeling he was familiar with. He had been so desperate to excel; now, even that was knocked out of him. The drive to excel was gradually dissipating, leaving him a dry, empty husk of what he used to be. He was giving up—giving up on the hope of doing better, of being happy.

As if reaching out one last time, even knowing it would never reach her, John sent his mother a small text message. She wouldn't understand it, like his whole life. It would be too late, since she spent all day at work. She wouldn't have the time to check on him, like always. He penned a small text that read: *"Bye, Mom."*

As soon as he sent it, he regretted it. *What am I doing?*

John shook his head, as though trying to shake down the myriad of thoughts that clouded and plagued his mind. *Okay. Get home. Get home. Talk this through with your mother in the kitchen. She will give you the audience this time if she understands the severity of the moment and how you feel. She has to. If she really loves you, she will make time. She'll pull off her old blue canvas shoes, ease herself into a kitchen chair, and wrap her hands around a mug of coffee. Then, we would talk. I'll explain the text. I will make her understand why the letter is catastrophic for me on top of everything else and how I can barely breathe with this consistent rejection.* Deep down, John knew he was thinking this way because he wanted to give his mother one last chance before he went ahead with this decision that he had made. *"How I'm losing my grip and willpower."*

It was the final straw in his many years of despair. It might not have seemed like a lot, but it was like adding gasoline to a pre-lit fire that had been burning for years inside of him.

His mother must have had no idea how much despair her youngest son had been feeling or how his constant failure, constant criticism from his brothers, and failure to form any close friendships had led him to this point. The whole truth was that John was tired. His whole being was exhausted by the loneliness eating him up from the inside out. The thought and idea of telling her this, of her making it all better, was overwhelming.

His mother's weary frown would soften as she listened to him pour out his heart. She would pat his knee and stroke his cheek like she did when he was a kid, when life was so much better and the hardships of reality didn't hit so hard.

John glanced up and saw a bus approaching. It was the bus that would take him home, dropping him only five blocks from their front door. He broke into a run and tried to flag the bus down, even though he wasn't at the empty stop, but the driver paid no heed as he indicated to turn off at the next street. As the vehicle drove away, John caught sight of the advertising banner on the side of the bus, above and below, through which bored faces gazed out at the world. The sign was for a company called "Murphy Auto."

Murphy Auto. John wanted to scream. It was as though the universe were mocking him by reminding him of Murphy University's rejection. John had a wretched sense of how obvious it was that he would miss the bus. Wasn't that just his luck? It was just the latest in a long line of bad luck; somehow, life was just waiting to kick him.

And with that playing on his mind, like a riddle with an answer that always just skips out of reach, John cut straight across the road to walk home. As he absentmindedly made his way across the busy road, a van startled him into reality as he almost collided head-on with it. With the horn of the van blaring from the hands of its angry driver, all the dazed John could see was the shocking message on the hood of the bright blue van:

"Hard work pays; never give up." John humorlessly snorted at the irony of that message.

He was seized by a hopeless emptiness, and suddenly, he just didn't care what had happened to him. He knew what he wanted to do. He knew what he had to do. He couldn't bear the burden much longer. The still-dazed young man staggered away from the van as more cars zipped around him like a deadly web that he was willfully walking into. He didn't care to look right or left. He could care less about the dozens of vehicles tearing along the asphalt. He was oblivious to the vans and cars that almost hit him. His ears were deaf to the cries and angry yells of the drivers. The blaring of the horns caused the shoppers and wanderers to look around and think him crazy for wandering in the road. John was no longer confused. He was a man with a mission. He knew what he had to do and knew he had to act fast. John picked up his pace, walking briskly like a Nitrogen-powered turbo human. He knew what he had to do.

7
WILD THOUGHTS

Eyes wide awake...
Restrained by wild thoughts.

Mary suddenly realized that the day was darkening and that the street lights had come on outside the kitchen window. Bars, nightclubs, and streets would be crowded soon, with young people moving and gathering to meet each other and have the time of their lives. "Why do I never, ever do that?" Mary asked herself. Helped by the alcohol, ambitions that she would have never entertained before emerged in her mind.

An idea was sprouting in her mind. Forming. Taking shape. Growing—whatever you wanted to call it—she knew she was walking down a road she had never walked before. Her blood started racing at the desire for light coursing through her veins. The gears in her head started turning as she started thinking about what she was about to do. If only Mary knew that this path she was heading down held doom for her. She stumbled slightly as she staggered back to her bedroom and grabbed the bottle of vodka again. It was warmer still and unpleasantly sour-tasting. Still, it was preferable to the rum, which had burned her throat earlier. Mary had never drunk this much alcohol before. In fact, she could hardly remember the last time she drank at all. As alcohol started to pass through her body, new feelings and reactions started to take over her body that she had never before experienced.

Is this what Lisa experiences every weekend she drinks?

More often than not, Lisa would bring a new male "friend" back with her, and they would disappear, laughing and tipsily clutching at each other, into her room, seemingly digging for gold—or spit—at the back of each other's throats. With the way Lisa behaved, one would easily mistake her for a floozy, but she was no lightweight academically either. She worked hard, but she never failed to have fun. How often had Lisa asked Mary to join her and Angelica when they hit the bars on the weekend? Mary had never responded positively to her offers. She knew that her father would never have approved of her going out to such things. Just the thought of her father finding her at a bar was terrifying. She hated the thought of what he might do to her when he was angry. She thought about that night and Elise Hart's stiff body. Mary shook herself. Her father has never hurt her and never will. She knew that, but it did not stop her from being less afraid. The last thing she needed to do was embarrass him or make him annoyed by partying or doing anything of that morbid sort. And aside from that, Mary usually worked towards her next goal—and there was always a next goal. Mary always did the maximum amount of work required of her, so even if she *wanted* to go out drinking and partying, she simply didn't have time.

What was the name of the bar they went to? Mary rubbed her aching head to clear her thoughts. Something Celtic?

Something Irish, maybe? "McMurphy's," she murmured. *That was it*. Angelica was always passing on stories about who was seen with whom at McMurphys, who had taken more drinks than they could handle, or who had cried in the lady's bathroom because their boyfriend had spent too long covertly admiring another girl. Oh, and lest Mary forget, there are the infamous stories about who dry humped who on the dance floor while Kesha was blaring through the bar. Yes, Angelica was that detailed. It turned out that pursuing that degree in journalism was a good fit for her. "What a dramatic world McMurphy's must be," Mary thought.

How come everyone else was out there having all the fun? A line from that old Bruce Springsteen song came to her: *There's something happening somewhere, baby I just know that there is.* That sense of anticipation and rush buzzed through Mary again. It was like her body knew something monumental was coming, but her mind simply couldn't see it.

Anyway, whatever was happening, wherever it was, it had all been happening to everybody else, and Mary had just sat up in her room, studying and waiting. For what? The next guy to come along and treat her like dirt? She took another swig of her liquid companion and grimaced. Sure, she'd had boyfriends. They went to the movies, to dinner, and wherever else. Guys had always approached her with the utmost respect, knowing she wasn't the kind of girl to dance widely in bars. They knew she was a little plain, so they acted accordingly. Of course, it wasn't like Mary thought she was particularly better than them, considering they knew how to have fun and she didn't. Once these "boys" had earned her trust and got to know her, they'd pick up on her lack of self-esteem and exploit it, sometimes unknowingly, but many times—many, many times—knowingly. Hey, the world is a cruel place.

Mary had never gone to a bar and picked up a man. She had always recoiled at the thought of it. Girls like her didn't do that kind of thing. Did they?

Swaying slightly and bringing the bottle of wine to her lips, Mary felt a pang of bitterness. Why was she always behind closed doors? Why wasn't she ever permitted to go out and have some fun? Waiting for the right guy wasn't working out so well, was it? These thoughts drifted through her mind and out. Mary could recognize that she was having an epiphany. A drunken, twisted, and slightly delusional epiphany—but weren't those the best kinds? Mary exhaled sharply through her nose.

Her fine upstanding boyfriend had decided that, frankly, Mary wasn't fun enough, so he hadn't hung around for long. He'd gone and found someone else—a leggy, dark-haired beauty who majored in history. He just lacked the decency to inform Mary about it beforehand. In fact, Mary had a sneaking feeling that Mark might even have met his new gal pal at McMurphy's. Damn McMurphy's.

"Why not me?" Mary asked out loud. "Why not me?" "Ugh! This pity party is not doing me any good!" Yet here she was, several hundred gallons of alcohol later, barely thinking straight, having the biggest pity party of all time.

While the unusual amount of alcohol Mary had consumed that day had dulled some of her senses and circuits, it seemed to have eased others open. Thoughts that Mary wouldn't typically have had started to cloud her mind. The tight rein she kept on her emotions seemed to ease, and comprehension came rushing in.

All the insecurities and self-doubt that plagued Mary, which informed her relationship with everyone and caused her to always be a "good girl," all came from other people's expectations of her.

There was a whole world of things and experiences that Mary had rejected just because she thought her parents—well, her father (Miriam didn't particularly care)—might disapprove of them or say that they would project the "wrong" image. Grayson Hart would have Mary's head on a law textbook if she ever made the mistake of bringing shame to his name.

Stunned by what was starting to dawn on her, she spun around to look at herself in the full-length mirror. Large eyes darkened by exhaustion and shadowed by the ceiling light stared back. "You, dumb idiot. You let them control everything about you." The irony of being controlled and unable to speak up for herself wasn't lost on her. How could she expect to be able to stand up and defend clients in a courtroom if she couldn't even defend herself? Mary chuckled humorlessly. How could she appear strong and capable in other people's eyes when she felt like such a sham? A very weak sham at that.

Then, there was her father, micro-managing her achievements and successes as though she were a puppet in his puppet show, even though she knew his dirtiest secret and knew that he was not as perfect as he or everyone else believed. He gave or withdrew love and affection according to whether or not Mary had pleased him, as though he was not the one who deserved to be under pressure and scrutiny for the rest of his life. Throughout her life, Mary was aware that her father loved nothing more than success. Although it had never been said out loud, she strongly suspected that if he had to choose between Mary and his reputation, Grayson Hart would look apologetically at his only child and save his name. He certainly has a chunk of dirt to protect his name from.

"Thanks, daddy. Thanks a lot," Mary whispered, smiling without much humor. She sipped from the bottle this time, her idea from earlier growing. *There's something happening somewhere, baby I just know that there is.* The creeping effects of the alcohol were washing through her, and she felt herself sliding slightly; her thoughts seemed slow in coming but then came with a rush towards her. The more she drank, the more she seemed to have glimpses of truth—or was that just the drink? Mary didn't know anymore. She would, though, soon enough.

She imagined her father's reaction if he saw her in her current state. He would be disgusted at the sight of her. The thought shuddered through her. Mary never saw Grayson Hart drink besides the odd glass of vintage wine with important clients or contacts. She had never seen him get drunk or lose control. He was perfect like that. On the other hand, she was no Grayson. She wasn't even good enough to be his daughter, she mused.

Mary had known privilege all her life. She always had nice clothes, riding lessons, a beautiful home, and vacations on the most exotic beaches around the world. She wanted nothing. If it could be bought, then Mary probably had it. She remembered becoming friends with the daughter of one of the Hart family gardeners, Jessie.

"You're lucky to have all of those clothes, Mary." Jessie had once said, staring into Mary's closet. Something in the way she said it made Mary's skin prickle slightly. Just the gentlest intonation made her sentence sound as though something was missing from the end of it. Something along the lines of "she might be lucky to have nice dresses, but..." Mary couldn't be sure, but it sounded like Jessie, dressed in her ice cream t-shirt and living in one of the poorer neighborhoods, felt sorry for her. Why would poor Jessie from the so-called bad side of town feel sorry for her? Didn't Mary have everything? *"No, you don't."* The voice was sharp and icy. *"Jessie has a mother who does her laundry and does her hair for her."* Mary shuddered violently. The last time she saw her mother was her limp body on the precious maroon rug in her parents' room. *"No,"* Mary thought, *"I don't have everything."*

Now, I have this place at college that I worked so hard for, this so-called pretty face, and this clever brain of mine. The thought was a depressing one. Throughout her life, Mary had everything she needed, and it amounted to nothing. Without the dread of her gradual zombie march to an unfulfilled life, the horrors of her childhood, and the one night that ruined it all, Mary was nothing but an empty waste of space. In a way, it made her feel guilty and ashamed that she had everything on the outside, but her inside was filled with emptiness.

That idea that had licked at the back of her mind a short time ago suddenly took hold. *There's something happening somewhere, baby I just know that there is.* In a half-daze, Mary quickly got up as if a light bulb had turned on in her head, and she headed for Lisa's room.

She threw open Lisa's closet the way Jessie had opened hers all those years ago in her room as a kid. Lisa had three hanging shelves suspended from the clothes rail, and each section was jammed with various clothing items. From a quick inspection, most were small and tight, and a surprising number had glitter on them. It was the exact opposite of Mary's neutral, conservative wardrobe. The emerald dress she'd bought for that disastrous date with Mark had been the brightest and most daring thing in her closet by a thousand miles.

Mary pulled out a bandage dress that was low-cut, clingy, and just about long enough to cover her underwear. It was bright, almost neon pink—the kind of thing Mary wouldn't ever be caught dead in.

Tearing off her oversized sweater, Mary wriggled into the dress. She fell over twice, partly due to the amount of alcohol coursing through her veins and partly due to the impossible nature of the dress. Finally, she got it in place. She hoisted it up to cover her cleavage and then realized that wasn't the idea at all. If she was doing this, she had to do it right.

"No way. I'm a bad girl tonight," thought Mary, her dark blonde hair falling over her face. She bit her lip. That tiny voice in her head, which had been silent for a while now, suddenly piped up. *Oh, Mary, this isn't the answer. Put on your pajamas, make a hot cup of cocoa, and try to get some sleep.*

"Shut up," said Mary out loud to that tiny voice. If it worked for everyone else, why not her? Lisa and Angelica came back from McMurphy's laughing and happy. Why shouldn't she? Didn't her boyfriend just dump her for another woman? So maybe it was, in fact, time for her to start acting a little wild. *Let's face it: being the good girl hasn't exactly done anything for me, has it?*

Taking another mouthful of the warm, sour wine from the bottle, Mary stared at her reflection; her sunken eyes were now washed out and tear-stained. That would never do. She lurched into Angelica's room, where she plopped herself down in front of Angelica's dressing table mirror. Pulling open the drawer, Mary found Angelica's makeup stash.

"Excellent. Just what I need," Mary felt a buzz of excitement. Her true, authentic self had never been good enough for anyone. "So, let's try tweaking it up a bit," Mary said softly as she started to apply some powder and highlight on her cheeks. She sometimes wore a little makeup, but nothing like this. She penciled in her brows, which made her look fierce but left her eyes almost invisible. So, she lined them thickly with a kohl pencil and smudged it with her finger. She flicked on two coats of mascara, finally giving her lips an angry slash of pillar-box red lipstick. A look that she had constantly seen on famous actors and celebrities on the red carpet and in magazines. "Let's give them what they want," Mary said with a little smirk.

"Hello, you." Mary's voice sounded different, from another place or another person. The stranger in the mirror smiled. She knew exactly what kind of guys would be attracted to this new her. The type that would hurt her. The ones who just want to get between her legs and do the whole "smash and dash" thing. The ones who saw a girl in a dress like this with a face like this and knew they didn't have to worry about having to meet the folks in a month. Hell! They didn't even have to stay the night. Mary shuffled the dress down even further and pouted in front of the mirror.

Maybe I can do even better than this. Swigging more wine and giggling uncontrollably like a little girl, she wandered back to Lisa's room and grabbed more clothes from the closet. "I'm positively overdressed!" she giggled as she held up a tiny skirt made from sequins and a net, as far as she could tell. She pulled the dress off and tugged on the skirt. "Ah, sparkly!" she smiled as she rewarded her efforts with a mouthful of wine. A top that was little more than a bra, a tight t-shirt, and a pair of hot pants in gold latex. Mary tried them all and then had a gulp of wine after each one.

At one point, she was aware that tears had started slipping from her eyes, smudging her new makeup, but she didn't really care. She didn't care about any of it anymore. Wild thoughts started to crowd in on her, and Mary was laughing and crying at the same time. The hysterics were unbelievable. She was horrified and disgusted with herself, yet she couldn't help bursting out in bitter laughter when she whirled around in another of Lisa's outfits.

Then she stopped and went to Angelica's room again, where she silently and grimly applied even more makeup until she could barely recognize herself. Her hair was wild. She looked awful, like the worst kind of girl who frequented the sleaziest kinds of bars. And yet, as disgusted as she was with herself, there was a raw energy about it that she hadn't felt in years, maybe ever. *"Is this freedom?"* Mary thought. *"Is this what freedom feels like? Not to care what anyone thinks? To just do what you want?"* The idea that she was on the cusp of freedom was momentarily as intoxicating as the alcohol.

Suddenly, Mary's phone rang. She looked down out of curiosity, and it was her stepmother calling. She instantly pressed to ignore the call. She didn't want anyone, especially her stepmother, to mess up this illuminated and carefree mood with which she was currently intoxicated. Then the woman called back almost immediately. Mary pressed "ignore" again. *"What the hell does Miriam want from me?"* Unbelievably, her stepmother called back a little over five times, and Mary ignored the call each time. Had Mary known that that call might have been the determinant of whether or not her life would uncontrollably spiral after that night, she probably would have put down the makeup brush and pressed "Accept." Mary, however, did not know. The calls remained unanswered.

Mary imagined her stepmother, knees pressed together, immaculate appearance, still the perfect Southern girl, twirling the landline wire with one finger, trying to reach her stepdaughter. The phone rang again. This time, a close friend from high school, Sangeeta, helped. Mary hadn't spoken to Sangeeta in months, although they had exchanged emails and messages a couple of times. "Why was she calling now? *What is with the weird, unexpected calls tonight?"* She thought. Well, it didn't matter anyway; Mary wasn't about to speak with anyone, so she ignored the imploring ringtone. Trying to focus on the small buttons was a little tricky, but Mary managed to change the setting on her phone so that all calls would now be silent.

Just then, a text message came in from her stepmother. This was a relatively rare occurrence, and even in her emotionally heightened state, Mary was curious about what her stepmother wanted to say to her. *"Mary, I've been trying to call you. I'm worried. Please call me back. I love you so much. I need to talk to you; I have something important to tell you!"*

Her face was frozen in a slight frown as she stared at the little screen. All the other words were blurred out, and the edges of the world seemed to soften as the only thing in focus were the words "I love you so much." Mary read that line over again. What? How could this be happening right now? Really? Amid these dark hours, a message telling her that she is loved? Tears began to pour down her face as she couldn't control her emotions.

Someone loves me. Out there in the world, my stepmother is thinking about me and loves me. The messenger was strange, but the message was well received.

Mary's mind began to spin. How could her stepmother love her when she's such a letdown? She staggered in Lisa's platform heels over to the edge of the bed, and leaned weakly on it. Mary so wanted to feel strong. She felt like she was made of fractured glass—hard and shiny, somehow still in one piece, but the slightest knock would shatter her into a million fragments.

I don't deserve love. Even if you mean it, you're wrong to love me. I don't deserve it.

She deleted the jarring message from her stepmother and sent her a brief one. *"I'm busy,"* it read. Holding herself together, Mary saw one of the cards from the local cab company stuck around Angelica's dressing table mirror and called the number on one of the cards. The woman on the other end of the line said they wouldn't have any cars free for an hour or more. The second company she tried said the same thing.

Mary paused. Was this a sign? Should she take off the clothes, wipe the ridiculous makeup off her face, and have a long sleep to shake off her stupidity? She drank another mouthful of Chardonnay, and as she did, she spotted a third company card tucked away behind the others. Murphy's Cab Co. The name rang a bell in her head. *Why was that? What was troubling her about that name?* Goosebumps raced up and down her arms.

Something didn't seem right to her. Why did her skin prickle when she saw that company card? Despite her intuitive misgivings, Mary's fingers were already dialing the number. It didn't come as a surprise that Murphy's Cab Co could get a car to her in just 15 minutes. The man on the line had told her that usually there were no drivers operating around the area at this time of the night, but tonight, Mary was obviously in luck. *"Luck,"* Mary snorted.

Mary rubbed her arm as goosebumps raced up and down its length. Something wasn't right, or was she being paranoid? But she plowed on and gave the operator the address.

"Are you ready now, madam?" The operator's voice sounded thin and clipped.

"Yes, I'm ready," Mary replied, suddenly trembling but unable to pin down a reason.

The operator began to mumble some words to her, and Mary fought the urge to call out in a panicked impulse to wait. Before she could make the decision, the operator spoke. The cab was already on its way.

The unease still hadn't let up in her stomach as she prepared to go out. With the anticipation drumming through her body, Mary had no idea—she had no idea what those calls from Miriam and Sangeeta meant, what that cab meant, and what that sickening churning in her stomach meant. The whole night was drumming up to a big awakening, and soon, she would find out.

8
POINT OF NO RETURN

Unraveling dusty luggage of words,
Humming a melody to blow pain away

Finally, John was home. He had just walked his longest after missing his bus. He walked so much that he could have sworn that his house was somehow running away from him. It was such a long and lonely walk where many lost and sporadic thoughts permeated his mind and consciousness. Loneliness was not a strange concept to him anyway. After he passed the door, John looked around at the familiar place—a once bustling family home, now empty, stale, and forgotten. The marks on the doorframe etched to record the boys' height were still visible, a painful reminder to John that his brothers had grown and flourished while he had grown but floundered. The empty coat rack, faded wallpaper, and threadbare carpets were all tragic and left behind, just like John, who, unlike his siblings, had failed to escape. The house where he grew up... where hope depreciated by the day. John shuddered. He knew no one was home even before he called out. His mother would be out at her second job. There was no note. John was doubtful that she even noticed he wasn't in his room last night and probably didn't even care to check for him this morning. She wouldn't notice that he had been missing since the previous evening. They didn't have dinner together anymore, so it didn't even matter. Most of his dinners were leftovers, which he ate in the solitary confinement of his room.

He placed his cell phone on the table, convinced he didn't need it. Why bother? No one was concerned about him. No one had reached out to him. Why would they ever call him? John was extremely exhausted. The long walk had done quite a number on him, so he shuffled over to the fridge.

As he fetched himself a glass of cold water, he noticed a pile of mail on the table, along with bills, flyers, and other papers belonging to his mother. On top of the pile was a letter addressed to him. One eyebrow shot up.

John picked it up and saw that the postmark across the top was from Rumyph University. Rumyph was one of the top colleges in the country, and places like Rumyph University were among the most sought-after. Back when John had applied in a fit of hope and optimism, Rumyph had been the touchstone, the dream. The campus had looked so beautiful, and John had dared to imagine himself there, studying and learning while making real friends and looking forward to the rest of his life. This mail was unlike the others, which contained devastating rejection letters; it looked odd. The letter was in a large, heavier-than-usual envelope dressed up in the college's main vibrant colors, which created instant curiosity in John. John's heart started to race as his armpits prickled and his palms got sweaty. He held his breath unconsciously.

With his heart thudding in his ribcage, John hooked his thumb underneath the envelope flap and then stopped. What was the point? It's just one of those rejection letters. He couldn't bear another one of those. His spirit was dampened at the thought of it being another rejection. Even if it is, what difference would it make? John had his path set out now, as he had already made his decision a while back. The impact of what he planned to do would be catastrophic for his family. The effects would last for the rest of their lives, he hoped. They would remember him. At least, he hoped they would. They'd finally realize how bad the pain inside had gotten. Ironically, they might, at long last, get a little closer to understanding him. Maybe he secretly wanted them to hurt. John admitted it to himself. He wanted them to feel the pain he had been enduring and holding in for so long. The guilt of not being there for him would haunt their consciences. *"Yes,"* John thought.

John threw the letter back down on the table. If it was another rejection, then he wasn't in for it. He had a certain sense of equilibrium now, which more bad news would upset. It ultimately would change nothing, but in a strange way that few would understand, he felt dull happiness that he had made his decision. Any more bad news would just unbalance his mood. John's head was clear now—clear with purpose and vision.

John took the stairs to his bedroom and felt an overwhelming desire for the simplicity of happiness, the joy of waking up in his bed, happy and content, smiling at the thought of what the day might bring. John had never known that feeling.

Why can't I just be happy?

And just like that, his mood was ruined. John sank onto his knees in his boyhood room and sobbed for the dreams that could have been. Surrounded by relics of hope from his life—books from his studies, a smiling picture of him as a toddler, a college prospectus tossed casually on the bedside table—that offered promise and the life he yearned for.

His cheeks wet and his vision hazy from tears, John took out his bag from the bottom of his closet. His hands found the things he needed, and he packed up the bag, his heart heavy in his chest. Sitting on the edge of his bed, he caught sight of his reflection in the dusty mirror. He hated what he saw; no wonder no one else had any faith in him. Why him? Did God just assign difficulties to him from his creation? John recalled an incident at school when he was a little older than six and just starting to understand life's complexities and harsh realities.

With his little hand clutching his mother's warm one, John had seen a homeless man on the street, shaking a few pathetic coins in an old coffee cup. The homeless man's hands and face were looking tattered all over; he had a woolen hat pulled down over his ears and an overcoat pulled in at the middle with a length of rope. He barely looked up as people walked by; he just shook his cup of coins to get attention and, hopefully, some sympathy.

"Momma, why doesn't God give that man some money so he doesn't have to beg, or is he being punished for some sin he committed?"

His momma had looked down at him, kindly but wearily, for hadn't she heard these questions so many times before? "I wouldn't know if he is being punished for some sin, but God doesn't give out money, sweetie. He gives us the ability to make choices for ourselves so that we can take care of ourselves and our loved ones, and for those who can't take care of themselves, he gives the rest of us kindness to help them."

John thought about this for a second and looked at his mommy again. "So, why didn't we give that man some money then, momma, as God gave us kindness to do?"

John recalled his mother's mouth moving into a thin line and seeing her take a deep breath before answering. "Because momma's struggling to make enough money to keep you and your brothers, honey. There isn't anything left to be kind with right now."

"So, if we don't have any money, is it God's job to help? Will God know about the man and that we couldn't help him?" John was a sensitive child. He was feeling upset and confused by the conversation. It was a time when he explored all of life's questions and thirsted to understand everything.

His mother sighed and rolled her eyes as she rushed to the store—they had a busy day ahead of them. "Yes, John. God will know, and God will help him," she paused, "And us."

And now, sitting in his room, sobbing at the wreckage of his life and what he planned to do, John recalled that conversation for reasons unknown to him. Did God help that man? Did God send someone with a twenty-dollar bill to put into that man's coffee cup?

John started thinking about himself and this somewhat horrible decision he was ready to take. Had God heard or seen him at the churchyard? Was God listening in on his tears now, and if he was, "Then why won't You help me?" John burst out. No one was going to show up with a twenty for him—or anything at all.

He ran his fingers through his hair, and his eyes, heavily laden with tears, located the picture frame on the wall. The photograph showed him, his mother, and his brothers at a family wedding two years ago. They were all dressed in their finest, and his mother looked a little puffy with pride at being there with her three grown sons. *"Well, two of them, probably,"* thought John. He doubted that he had inspired too much pride in his mother's heart.

How will they feel when he carries out his plan? Will they cry? Will they miss him? Deep down, John knew they would finally take notice of him and that it would dawn on them that he couldn't carry around his burden of sadness and despair any longer.

"You won't forget me," John whispered to the photograph. "You will remember me, and you will talk about me, and finally, you will care."

Even if they all thought he was a terrible person and a coward for going through with it, it would be something. And John would be free. No more of this pain. No more rejection and despair so palpable that John sometimes felt it was written across his face.

The sudden sound of a crack of thunder tore through the quiet house. A few moments later, there was a flash of bright light across the sky and another peal of thunder. Drizzle began to pitter against the window.

The final insult. I have to do it in the rain. I'd imagined a calm evening and maybe even the last threads of light leaving or beginning in the vast expanse of sky.

If God had been listening at any point, He clearly wasn't in any rush to respond, that was for sure. John listened to the sound of the rain on the ground as it became intense, and he looked at it as it cast an atmosphere of gloom through the window, which somehow matched his mood. "Rain it is, then," John said softly. "So be it."

John scrambled through the books on his reading table to grab a pen and paper as he stumbled on a poem he had written on a piece of paper some months ago. The paper was crumbled, but he could still read the words on it:

I am a lone man in the ball,
Screaming my price for the happiness being auctioned,
But no one seems to hear my voice.
I feel like I'm drowning in the echo of my own voice.

Tears rolled down John's eyes as he read the sad piece. He realized that he still lived in the reality of the poem, but it didn't matter now; his voice was about to be heard.

John dropped the poem, tore a sheet from one of the books on the table, picked up a pen, and left his room without a backward glance. It did occur to him that if he looked back at that bright room, he might still sense the spirit of the happy little boy who once played there. That little boy's spirit wouldn't be allowed to talk him out of what he wanted to do.

Heading for the kitchen, John reminisced about the content of the letter. He had been mentally writing this letter for months, if not years. There were no wasted words, no accusations. Just a final attempt to let them all know how much pain he had been dragging around with him for a long time, like Marley's chains from the Christmas Carol.

There was no real respite now, where once there had been. John had reached his tipping point, his point of no return. He wanted his mother and brothers to know that he was sorry for any hurt this would cause them, but he knew they would have each other. "I'm so sorry, Momma," John whispered as he placed the letter into an envelope and left it on the kitchen table, next to those papers and bills, the ordinary bits of life, and his letter. *"To you,"* he had written on the front.

John grabbed his jacket and felt his awareness heighten at all the final things he was doing now that the letter was on the kitchen table, waiting for his mother to read it. Anticipation drummed in his spirit, making every step more significant than the last. Walking down the hallway and opening the front door, he heard the loose pane in the porch shudder slightly in its frame as he closed the door behind him for the last time. He could not stop the tears now. He had spent a long time bottling up the tears. Now he could cry at the life he would never have. He knew he would soon be free, and that in itself was happiness for him, but he felt such deep discomfort at what he was leaving to his mother and brothers.

John turned to walk down the familiar street. How many times had he run down this pavement, carefree and unaware of how life would change? It was hard to pinpoint the time that it had started to change. John had been aware of a shadow within him since he was around 10 years old or so. He imagined it as an oily puddle. Whenever someone said something hurtful to him or if he felt he'd failed somehow, the pain would somehow be absorbed by this shadow inside him. In turn, the shadow grew, and by the time he reached his teens, John knew that the puddle had become a river, but the larger it became, the less able he was to tell anyone about it. Oh, how desperately he wished he could have talked to someone and unloaded all his distress. He could have communicated his sorrow, but there was never anyone there, so this shadow grew exponentially without stopping—absorbing, growing, absorbing, growing, and so on.

And now, walking down that street on this day, he glanced up and saw his mother's car approaching. He almost didn't recognize it at first, as the vehicle traveled much faster than his mother habitually drove.

By some stroke of great misfortune, Eleanor Ribeaux had been involved in more than one road traffic accident, mainly shunts and curb-grazing, except for the last one, two winters ago. Eleanor had just left one of her jobs at a local upscale supermarket and decided to take a different route home as the snow was starting to fall and her usual route was vulnerable to drifts and roadblocks.

She was only one mile from home when Matthew Leonard, a driver for Phurmy's Electrics, suffered a heart attack at the wheel of his company van. The out-of-control vehicle had careered across the lane where Eleanor was approaching and clipped her wing, forcing her off the road and into the concrete supports of the flyover. Eleanor's injuries had been bad but not life-threatening. She had received some compensation from Phurmy's insurance company, but it didn't cover all of the costs of her hospital stay, nor did it account for the debts that Eleanor had accumulated while she couldn't work. She had just enough compensation to buy another car, which was essential for Eleanor to be able to go to work at her various jobs. Without a car, she could hardly work or take the kids to the places they needed to be. She didn't have the kind of jobs that allowed for long periods of absence, even if it was because a runaway company van had smashed her up. Eleanor had the additional misfortune of hiring a lawyer who didn't recover all the money she was entitled to and was eventually struck off. However, by that time, Eleanor didn't have the inclination or energy to pursue a further case for misconduct and negligence against her former lawyer, who probably should never have practiced law in the first place.

Eleanor began to work more intensely, thinking that she was doing all she could to keep her family together in new shoes, new clothes, and a home, all without noticing that her work was gradually taking her attention away from her family. The two older boys were able to manage. But John was different. He just saw his mother drifting further away—never there, always too busy to take any notice of him.

Whatever else the accident left her with, she developed an aversion to driving but couldn't avoid it because she had to get to work. When Eleanor did drive, it was slowly and cautiously. She had never been a poor or inconsiderate driver, but now she was almost as much of a liability on the road as some speeding kid with a freshly printed license. Such was her extreme caution and determination to drive somewhere slightly under the speed limit.

So John was taken aback when he noticed his mother's car moving faster than he had seen it in the previous two years. The car approached, and John was transfixed, momentarily distracted by his mother's arrival and the manner of it. And then, John felt his heart plummet as she simply drove past. He released the breath he didn't know he was holding. Had he hoped for her to stop or notice him? No, he was too fixed on his path for that, but *"still, you're my mother!"* John screamed inside.

At the end of the line, he was desperate, crying outside his boyhood home with sorrow that he couldn't articulate, and his mother drove past him. She hadn't even seen him. *"That's how much anyone cares,"* John thought bitterly. A mother's love is unconditional and unending, supposedly. And she hadn't even noticed him.

John would not have imagined that he could hurt more, but his mother, driving by, twisted the knife already lodged in his heart.

The rain was falling in a much softer manner now, making the evening both fragrant and dull. The droplets became one with his tears. His resolve was complete; the years of that black river inside him destroyed his dreams, hopes, and much more. John walked on towards the terrible fate he had always known would be his. There was no going back for him now. This was it. This was it.

9
A GOOD TIME GIRL

Behind every glorious facade
there is always hidden
something broken and in despair.

Mary stumbled towards the front door, checking herself out in the hallway mirror. She could barely recognize herself; the makeup was thick and poorly applied, and her hair was a mess. Her roommate's clothes presented her as the antithesis of the image she usually tried to conjure up. The good girl was gone—long gone behind her.

Mary almost wanted to give herself a new name for her new identity. Then Mary could be hidden away completely, with her tiny voice lost inside this new, brash girl who was unafraid to hit the bars in town and have a good time. "A Good Time Girl." Mary remembered her mother saying that phrase through pursed lips. "The Good Time Girls were no better than they ought to be."

"Well, Mommy, tonight your little girl is going to have a good time." Mary blew a kiss to her reflection, leaving a garish

red lipstick blot on her fingertips. Tonight, Mary was going to do exactly what she felt was right for her. For the first time, she was going to shrug off what everyone thought she should do. She didn't want to give a crap about her father and his rules, expectations, and secrets.

Everything about tonight—how she looked, the new character she put on, what she planned to do—would utterly horrify her father. A wave of dark anger formed in her chest, and Mary felt her face go warm at the thought of her father's control over her all these years. How long had Mary been half aware that she barely existed as a person in her own right when it came to Grayson? She was an appendage, an accessory to his success. Mary's standing in his eyes was directly related to how good she made him look. Her reward was knowing her father was proud of her. *How proud would you be now, dad? Looking like a "Good Time Girl" with the morals of an alley cat? Would you still love me now, dad?*

Mary was hazily aware that she was about to place herself in an incredibly vulnerable position, looking as she did, with a plan to be the easiest girl in the bar. She wouldn't be selective; oh, no, no time for that. This was the night rules got broken. Mary had a hunger to be wild and free for once in her life, brought on by her despair and helped by alcohol.

She thought, *"Maybe what I'm looking for is what I deserve."* To be used, treated badly, and thrown away. A disposable encounter. *"That's all I'm good for, but it won't be me this time. I'm someone else tonight."*

"And tomorrow night?" That tiny voice inside that Mary thought had been silenced suddenly spoke up. *"Who will you be tomorrow night? Which Mary will sober up in the morning?"*

"Interesting question," Mary admitted to herself. She had no idea who she would be tomorrow; tonight would have to do for now, and she was going to have some fun. Giddy with the alcohol she had consumed, Mary tripped as she left the house, and as she did, a faint drizzle settled on her face and hair. It felt real, pure, and refreshing. The unexpected freshness and soft touch of the droplets on her skin affected Mary in a way she would never have expected. Fresh tears sprang to her eyes, but not the hot, desperate tears of earlier that evening, but sad, poignant tears that seemed to well up from a childlike part of her. The sweet and unexpected joy of rain on her face made her sadder than she had ever been; such was the contrast with the shadow within her.

Then bitterly, she recalled how the television in her room had been on all day as she lay unable and unwilling to switch it off, not being able to move and feeling paralyzed on the bed. She remembered the weatherman, John Murphy, giving out the report in his familiar, local accent and telling everyone to have a terrific day and evening as there was no risk of rain at all. "Don't bother with a jacket today, folks!" he had winked at the end of his report. And yet, the rain became a little heavier and settled on Mary's exposed arms. "Dear Mr. John, you lied," she sarcastically said to no one in particular.

"Of course, it's raining." Mary felt a tight and humorless smile touch her lips. "It's my night out. My special night," she mused out loud. "Of course, it would rain."

The car she had ordered pulled up by the curb, and the friendly-looking cab driver gave her a breezy smile. Mary opened the door and dropped heavily and clumsily into the rear of the cab. The driver looked with concern at his passenger. He knew she was a mess and wondered what advice he would have to give tonight.

"Where are you headed? A pretty lady like you must mean you're heading somewhere nice." The driver said this while looking at Mary in the mirror with a polite smile.

"McMurphy's Bar, please." Mary didn't give the driver an eye as she spoke. Mostly, she felt that anyone who would compliment her was some sort of creep or a bad person.

The driver, Joe, shrugged and said, "Okay, wherever the pretty lady wants to go, I'll take her." He wasn't in a position to tell her that the last place on earth she should be going to was McMurphy's Bar since it was a dirt bar. That place was troubled at the best of times, and this young woman didn't seem capable of handling a harsh word, never mind the treatment she might receive at McMurphy's. Joe couldn't help but worry about this woman. Joe knew he couldn't cross a line with his customers, but this woman needed a bit of kindness and a helping hand.

He saw a lot of his niece, Rose, in this young woman—the wide eyes frantically asking for help, the shrunken figure showing how much she struggled to keep it together, and the most disturbing thing of all, the jumpy look that showed that she was at the end of the line. This young lady was a quiet and mysterious beauty, yet she dressed in a way that didn't sit right with her beauty and aura. Joe sighed inwardly. Being young was tough; he was aware of that fact, especially at times like this. It was so different from when he grew up without the internet and social media. His heart ached slightly for this young woman.

As the cab sped through the streets, which now glistened with rain, Mary looked at all the people strolling with loved ones, holding onto each other, arm in arm. She noted bitterly the fathers holding tightly to their daughters' hands as they crossed the street—not out of control or firmness, but with love and tenderness. Everyone looked so happy, so complete in their little scenes of contentment. *Do they know how lucky they are?* She longed for some of that closeness, the warmth of knowing someone really loved her. She had a quick flash of the message from her stepmother, telling her that very thing, but dismissed it just as quickly as it came. She wasn't even sure she believed it. What did Miriam, the mannequin, know about love?

Mary turned her attention back to the people in the street. Why couldn't she be that happy? They didn't even seem to mind the rain. She could no longer bottle up the anger that built up inside as she suddenly wound down the glass and screamed out, "Can't you see it's raining? It's a filthy night; go home and keep your happiness there, not out here where it kills me to see it." She got no response from outside, as nobody could have heard her due to the rain. However, Joe only shook his head, pitying the poor young lady. He was right; there was a lot of pain in this one.

Mary slumped back in her seat, her irrational envy for the people in the street dissipating along with her disquiet at their apparent contentment. They were entitled to it. "They were probably good people," she reasoned. She suddenly felt confused, perhaps because of the wine or perhaps because of what she was doing, sitting in this cab, covered in awful makeup. Her skirt had ridden up as she had thrown herself in the back of the cab, and she plucked at the fabric to cover her thighs more. But that wasn't the idea, right? Wasn't she supposed to enjoy looking like this?

A wave of dark sadness hit her as she thought of all the different things that had brought her to this point. Her father.

Her so-called boyfriend. *"They should see me now,"* she thought. At the thought of Mark, a wave of anger rose inside her. Words slipped out of her mouth as though she were unaware of them. She didn't mean to start speaking out loud, but the feelings were powerful, and she couldn't contain them. She mumbled at first, reliving moments of sadness and humiliation, particularly last night's humiliation. Then she started raging about the unfairness of how men think they can treat women as they please, without regard for their feelings. Mary was so incensed by the evil that men could commit and the wreckage that they left in their wake that she even told Joe, driving his cab and trying to keep out of trouble, that he was just as bad as the rest of them.

Joe kept his mouth in a thin line and focused solely on the wheels. He wasn't angry with the young woman. He'd been at the cab-driving game for too long to take offense at the odd insult. He felt sorry for her even more. The way the young woman was here wearing a face, outfit, and attitude that she obviously wasn't comfortable in, while rambling about how everyone had hurt her too much, struck a personal chord with him. Joe knew a bit more about that life than Mary could have guessed, and he wished she would change her mind and ask him to drive her home. On this night, Mary was too similar to the way Joe acted when he was her age.

Mary suddenly started patting the seat next to her and checking her bag. She couldn't find her phone and knew she wanted it, though she wasn't entirely sure why it was so important to her. "Please turn around; I need to get home. I left my phone at home. Take me home now. I need to go now!" Mary flew into a panic. She so wanted to set herself free, and it seemed obstacles were being thrown at her to prevent her freedom.

Joe looked at her in the mirror, starting to feel mildly agitated with how she was yelling at him, but saw with a pang how her makeup was already halfway down her face, carried there by her tears, and he held up a hand to indicate that he'd got it; they were turning around. He kept thinking of how and if he could give her advice to make her feel better. After all, he took great pride in helping out with problems and any sort of hardship a customer encountered.

Mary settled back into her seat and adjusted her legs to feel more comfortable. As she did so, she kicked something on the floor. Her phone! She reached down and closed her hand around it. "Wait, it's okay! I have my phone. Can we drive back to the bar now?" Her voice was unnaturally animated, and she sensed that some of the effects of the alcohol were starting to wear off slightly, even though she was still highly intoxicated. "That wasn't good," she reasoned. She didn't want to be aware of her actions. She needed to drink more quickly, or she risked losing her nerve. The darkness and sensibility started to leave, and she didn't want them to.

Joe, the patient man he was, sighed heavily, trying to box up his annoyance. He wanted to help her, but with her anger and outbursts of drunken nonsense, he started to feel like she was a hopeless case. Making a turn at the end of the block, Joe couldn't avoid getting stuck in a one-way with no means of turning out of it. The cab was in a flow of traffic, waiting to make two more turns around the upcoming block to double back, when Mary felt the anger she had felt earlier rise again.

Yet another obstacle had been thrown in the way of her trying to find some freedom and satisfaction. Being stuck in this endless line of stationary traffic just illustrated perfectly how she would never be able to find the happiness she craved. This was symbolic of her life. The happiness she innately and desperately wanted had become a long, congested road with traffic and seemed less reachable. Everyone else would be able to go out and have fun while she, Mary Hart, sat in a cab in a traffic jam, watching everyone else enjoy themselves.

"This is not fair. Why me again? Why am I stuck here while all of those people are out having fun? Why not me? Why not me, just once?" Mary raged inside, and suddenly it burst out of her. She kicked the seat in front of her and screamed at Joe, "Go a different way. You're a driver; find a different way! Why are you just doing nothing?" She felt hot and could hear a screaming sound, not even making words, and she realized that it was coming from herself. She didn't even recognize herself anymore.

Joe took a deep breath, trying to calm his nerves that were being trampled upon, and also wanting to help this troubled young woman get a grip on herself. "I'm sorry, ma'am, but the traffic is bumper to bumper here, and I cannot make the turn back onto Main Street. If you can just try to settle back there for a few more minutes, we'll be out of..."

Joe's words were lost as Mary cut across him with a scream that pierced the air. "Oh my gosh!" The rain suddenly thwacked into the side of the cab like a fist as the heavens opened. The rain pounded the pavements. A deep, guttural rumble of thunder competed with the relentless drive of the rain, and everyone was suddenly running for cover.

Mary halted for a moment, her anger and internal storm quieted by the dramatic burst of the weather. "Isn't there another way to the bar beside Main Street, like an alternative route or something?" Mary realized they were now closer to the bar than they were to home, and she had no intention of changing her plans. The old Mary came back just then for a moment, and she added in a softer voice, "Please?"

Joe glanced up into the rear-view mirror and saw her eyes—sad, pleading, and plaintive. He was getting tired and a little annoyed now, but his patience served him well in situations like this. "Yes, ma'am. We could take the Murphyne Bridge, but it will take, I don't know, maybe 15 minutes longer. Waiting this out will get us there quicker."

But Mary was on her last nerve and couldn't bear to be stationary. She didn't care if it took longer; she needed to feel like she was moving forward and getting closer to her goal instead of staying in one spot like this. "Take the bridge." Her voice was flat. She wasn't going to negotiate this.

"But, ma'am, I promise, if we just wait for five min..."

"I said, take the bridge. Take the bridge now. Now!" Mary's voice was shrill and nearly hysterical.

Finally, Joe was unnerved by the strange young woman in his cab. It was with intense discomfort and a curious sense of foreboding that Joe pointed his cab in the direction of the Murphyne Bridge. Mary kept getting restless, like a bomb was about to go off. *"This is it. This is it."*

10
GUILT

Like a wolf in the night,
Chasing earnestly at my heels,
The guilt haunts me

Sean cursed to himself as he turned his newly bought car onto the familiar street. Why had he let things get this far? Life was a whirlwind of events—weekends with friends and weekdays working hard to build the life he'd always dreamed of. Somewhere along the line, your eyes just leave the ball somehow.

The houses had grown less salubrious with time, and the shops were less inviting over the last couple of miles. The three-bedroom house, which was now home to his mother and little brother, was firmly on the wrong side of town. Her financial credit was as unimpressive as the neighborhood, but what Eleanor Ribeaux lacked in means, she made up for in personality, and she had been able to talk the landlord into renting the house to her despite her poor line of credit and inconsistent income. To be fair, the landlord had never regretted it—the Ribeaux family made decent enough tenants, even with three big, strong boys knocking around the place and no father.

Sean didn't visit much. There wasn't much reason to. His mother was always busy, and his youngest brother... Sean and John hadn't really connected for years. Had he known? Sean's heart was racing. His mother had placed a call to him a couple of hours ago, distraught and desperate for Sean to come home as quickly as possible. The worst had happened. Eleanor had been almost hyperventilating on the phone, and it had taken several attempts before Sean actually got the full story about what had happened. He sighed heavily.

Sean's relationship with John had never been an easy one. Sean recalled a Halloween night when John was a little kid. His mind drifted slightly to that memory. Their mother had been working, as she always did. Sean and Jake were babysitting. They were peeved at not being able to go trick-or-treating with their friend, as John was too scared to step foot outside.

"C'mon, John. What kid doesn't like trick-or-treating? You are so weird." Jake had been really annoyed about missing out on his annual candy haul, and Sean wasn't far behind him.

John had curled up in a ball on the sofa, trying not to cry. He'd been wearing his Incredible Hulk pajamas, and he had looked so small and frail, nothing like his elder brothers. John had a slight build and was never going to be more than five feet eight in height. Sean and Jake had needled him all evening about allowing them to miss out on trick-or-treating and the fact that John wouldn't even open the door when other kids came by trying to score candy.

In the end, his brothers decided they would have fun by hatching a prank. Once Scooby-Doo had finished, they carried John to bed with one of his books and crept outside. Amid snuffled laughter and each telling the other to be quiet, Jake and Sean eventually managed to poke the end of the washing prop into the pumpkin that had been carved by the guy in the shop and left on the doorstep as the family's concession to the festivities. They carefully lifted the prop, the pumpkin swaying as they did so. With great care, the brothers managed to maneuver the carved face right in front of John's window.

Sean had moved the prop so that the pumpkin bumped against the window. When there was no response from John, they bumped the window harder. A small, unsuspecting hand had crept around the curtain edge and pulled it back a little. Sean could still see John's face, stricken with terror, clawing at his cheek with the other hand. He staggered backward and fell in a heap, crying and screaming, before scrabbling towards the door, shouting for his two big brothers to help him.

Sean and Jake had remained outside, almost crying with laughter at how well their prank had gone. Jake clutched his stomach as they rolled on the ground, congratulating each other on a prank well done. When John came outside to find them, he saw the pole, the pumpkin, and his brothers laughing. It had fallen into place for him quickly; even though he was a kid, John was smart. Sean winced as he recalled John's little face crumbling and his tears of hurt and humiliation.

Jake had stopped rolling around and giggling long enough to yell to John that he had done it to toughen him up and to stop behaving like such a big baby all the time. He poked fun at how often the younger boy ran crying to their mother.

John had reddened at those words. Was he a big baby and too sensitive? He wasn't aware that he went crying to his mother too much. He wanted to be like his brothers, and he felt ashamed and sad that a line was drawn in the sand with him on one side and his brothers on the other.

But hadn't John brought some of it upon himself, at least? He never hung out with friends or played sports with others. Sean recalled how his younger brother could never get along with anyone—girls or friends—in the usual easy way that his peers did. He was an awkward kid, and Jake and Sean hadn't made it any easier for him.

So, hadn't Sean let his little brother down? Wasn't he supposed to protect and take care of him like big brothers were supposed to? How about that? John's skinny stature, in his Incredible Hulk pajamas, haunted Sean as he approached the house where they'd all grown up. In the years that had slipped by, Sean had lost his harder shell, which he'd built around him after his father left. He could now look back and see how different things should have been.

Sean should have stood shoulder to shoulder with his kid brother, no matter how weird he was. Wasn't that what was causing the heavy pressure in his chest when he thought about John? Guilt? Wasn't it true that as soon as his mother started sobbing and pleading with him on the phone to come home, he felt responsible for letting John down and that it was all his fault somehow? His throat suddenly became parched and scratchy; his hands were cold and clammy, and his eyes were prickling.

Sean had never shared the hurt that he bore inside him since the year he left college. He didn't want to burden his mother, and Jake was at that time lacking much in the way of sensitivity, and anyway, it was Sean's burden, and that's just how it was.

In fact, his coping mechanism greatly informed his approach to John's problems. Sean had been able to suck it up and get on with his life. In his mind, that was John's path to take.

Sean went a little cold at the memory and switched down the blast of air conditioning in the car. He had been an idiot after college, hanging around with *"bad people with no future,"* as his mother would frequently call them, and getting into trouble he had no business being around. Somewhere in the midst of this, he started seeing a girl named Naomi. Naomi had black curly hair and a stunning wide smile that captivated Sean the moment he saw it. She was a waitress in a restaurant outside town and shared a house with three other sorority girls. She was happy with her life. They had gotten to know each other pretty well over the summer, and by the end of it, Naomi told Sean that she was pregnant. Sean had gone into shock and was searching for a way to cope with this new burden.

He couldn't inform his mother about it; she had told him time and time again about how to avoid this very situation. Sean didn't trust Jake to keep the secret from their mother, and anyway, Jake would be no help. Sean did what he thought he would never do: he called his father. His father wasn't a stranger to him after all, even if he wasn't there all the time. They had met up a couple of times without his mother's knowledge, seen each other around, and even attended a couple of family get-togethers once or twice. He never really left town but tarried for some reason and, out of all his boys, stayed in contact with Sean. On the other hand, Sean had never thought of his father as a confidant or someone to turn to. Maybe this was a turning point in his life in more ways than he thought.

The day Sean met his father downtown for a glass of beer and to share what he thought was a disaster was hot and unforgiving. The pavement shimmered before him as he pushed open the heavy door to Raymond's Bar. His father was occupying a bar stool, one eye on the TV and the other on the pretty barmaid. Sean didn't think much of his father, but he had lived a fairly varied life, and he needed some advice from someone, and to be honest, he missed having a father figure in his life.

Sean told his story as his dad listened. He even asked the odd question: Was Naomi pretty? Did they have a future together? The thing was that the more Sean talked about Naomi, the more he realized he really did like her. Maybe he even loved her. Sean didn't want Naomi to be pregnant, at least not yet. However, she was, and it was his responsibility. Then his dad knocked back another drink and turned to face Sean full-on.

"You really do like this Naomi girl, yeah? I think you should stand by her; maybe you should. But you know what? It's pretty easy these days for her *not* to be pregnant, if you catch my drift." Sean's father adjusted on his barstool and crossed one leg over the other in a gesture that would have seemed vaguely feminine, were it not for the aura of slightly unignorable masculinity that his father surrounded himself with. "You know what?" His dad threw the last of his drink down his throat and swallowed the alcohol. "I wish I'd managed to persuade your mother to have, you know, not been pregnant a couple of times."

Sean blinked at his father. Had he misunderstood him? Was he really saying what Sean thought he was saying? Emotions that could cause him to cry—or scream—ran through his nerves, but hell would freeze over before Sean let this man see him cry. Sean stood up, his legs feeling weak but his jawline firm. "The best thing you ever did for our family was to leave it." He grabbed his jacket and made for the door. He heard his father's mocking, drunken call after him as he left. Sean didn't bother to listen. That wasn't a man worth listening to.

Naomi hadn't been pregnant. It had been a blip, a mistake. They dated for a while longer and then stopped seeing each other as the chill of winter bore down on them. No hearts were broken, and Naomi went on to marry someone else, and they had a pretty good life together, which was more or less what she deserved.

Those words and lifelong actions from his father overshadowed so much of Sean's life from that point on. He became driven and ruthless for a while, then self-pitying and ill-tempered, asking, "Was he a mistake?" But he came through it all, and he wanted John to beat his demons, as he had fought his. Sean had worked long hours to be successful. Sean never wanted to be scrambling for money—he needed to feel as though he had a safety net beneath him. Now he had money, and it was due to his own hard work. But at what cost?

Sean pulled up in front of the house, raced up the driveway, and felt the bunch of keys rattling around in his pockets the way they had since he was twelve and allowed to carry the keys around. The door was wide open, only hinting at the chaos he was about to find inside.

His mother was sitting alone at the table, her eyes streaming with tears. She was berating herself and close to being hysterical. Eleanor grabbed her son and pulled him towards her, clutching his shirt like a thief at a supermarket. She thrust a piece of paper at him that was softened and blurred with tears. "Look, look. This is what I found when I got home from work. I found it on the table, Sean. It was just lying there, Sean. Just lying there."

Sean took the letter from her shaking hand and read it. His heart felt like a cold fist had just closed around it and was squeezing hard with evil intent. An icy dryness lined Sean's throat, and his hands trembled. "Oh no. Oh no. This can't be happening." Sean's voice seemed to be echoing down a corridor. "No, no," he murmured, staring beseechingly at his mother.

Suddenly, Eleanor started to take deep, fast breaths and then went limp. Her face went blank in an instant when she collapsed onto the chair. She pounded on her chest with her fist and tried to grab a breath. Sean yelled, "Breathe, mom, breathe!" Sean gathered every bit of his strength to keep from succumbing to his own panic. His mother was crying and barely drawing breath between her racking sobs. Finally, she managed to breathe, and Sean almost collapsed with relief when he saw some color return to her face as the oxygen flooded her bloodstream.

"I did this to him! It's all my fault; I should've been around more; I should've shown more love." His mother's voice was a wail of lament. "But I do love him; I love you all. It's just been so hard raising you boys."

Sean cut her short. "I know, mom. We had to do what we had to do."

Eleanor flashed him a look of recognition and then sobbed again. "John is such a sweet kid. He was no trouble. He's different, that's all."

Sean had his arm around her, trying to offer what comfort he could, when his mother leaned forward to take an envelope from the table. "Look, I found this. It's addressed to John."

Sean saw that the letter was addressed to John and glanced cautiously at her. "Read it, read it," she implored. Sean opened the envelope and took out the thick, white, folded letter.

"Oh, my goodness." Sean's voice was flat, with a slight awe, but his reaction was not mistaken. "Oh, my God." He looked at his mother. "Did John see this?"

Eleanor shook her head. "No, it was sealed and in the trash. He didn't open it. I guess he thought it was just another letter, like all the others." Everyone knew about John's long train of rejection letters.

Sean picked up his keys quickly. "I'm going to look for him." The determination in his voice was thick and hard to miss. He would let go. He wouldn't let John go. He had to find his baby brother.

11
ABANDONED

This one sits in an empty room
Waiting and waiting
For the one who never comes

Mary stared hopelessly at the rear lights of Joe's cab as it vanished into the rain. That small part of her that tried to make its voice heard was mortified at how she had behaved in the cab. She had been rude and insolent, swearing and losing her temper for no reason, like a spoiled, petulant child. Finally, Joe had had enough. He was a good man, but he had his limits, and Mary had pushed him almost beyond what was reasonable. No advice that he could give could help her. She was lost.

As she stood there in the rain, Mary bit her lip to stop herself from crying. The cab driver had finally gotten fed up with all of her nonsense. He didn't say a word, which upset Mary even more. He simply stopped the cab, ignored all her ranting, and calmly walked around the car to the back seat passenger door. He opened the door and said nothing. He stood there in the rain and silently decided to finish his work for the night after getting rid of this troubled young lady and moving on to help someone else. Joe didn't plead with Mary; he just stood there, holding the door open, while she lashed out at him, screaming that he couldn't do this to her and that he had to drive her to the bar. A switch had flipped when the girl started to shout about how her daddy would sue him, how Joe was *nothing,* how he was a nobody, but her father was a hotshot lawyer who would ruin him.

Mary had lost all of Joe's sympathy, and the rambling pleas and threats fell on deaf ears. Some coherent part of her recoiled at how she had yelled at the disgruntled driver, "You don't know who I am. Do you know who my father is? He's the fiercest lawyer in the country; he'll sue you. I'll sue you. You'll never drive your stupid cab again."

Joe didn't say a word back to her. He was getting angry with her, but Joe was one of those men who became quieter when they were angry. It was a good way of keeping his temper, which Joe had learned over the years. He waited by the car door, getting drenched in the cold rain. Joe could feel the chill settling into his bones, but he waited patiently until the girl finally managed to get the message: she was not going any further in this cab tonight. Joe watched her register the memo and cast around for her bag with dejection. She carelessly grabbed her phone and bashfully attempted to pull down her short skirt as she exited the car with little grace. Joe had closed the passenger door and kept his head and eyes down as he walked back to the driver's side. He hesitated and then met her eyes for a moment. "Find someone to take care of, pretty lady."

Mary looked at him. Was it so obvious that no one cared about her? "I don't have anyone to take care of me," Mary spat back at him as the words stung her heart. Had she had a mother to love and care about her, those words would not have rung as true as they did.

Joe pushed his cap back further and started to climb into his cab. "No, *you* find someone to take care of. It might help with whatever you are going through. Good luck." And with that, he slammed the door and drove off. What nonsense was the man speaking? Mary's frazzled mind wondered as the cab sped off, leaving her and her crisis behind. Moments later, Mary was alone, her belongings bundled in her arms, her throat sore, and her mind whirling. By now, the buzz of the alcohol was wearing off. May regretted it instantly, as everything she was racing to avoid came at her almost like a flood. The tapestry of inebriation was slowly being unraveled, which did not bode well for the crying mess of a lady.

Why should she find someone to take care of? That wasn't the idea at all. She needed someone to tell her that they cared; she needed to be taken care of. The only guy she thought cared about her had left her. She felt utterly alone and used.

Still clutching her things, Mary started to walk slowly down the street. She vaguely recognized the route to the bridge, not too far ahead. She was a mess. She was aware that her makeup, which had been poorly applied, was now all over the place. Her hair was a nest of knots. She was getting wet and knew she would draw attention in the street and stand out as a wreck, maybe even the long-derided "Good Time Girl." Except she was patently not having a good time. At all.

A ball of anger began to form in her stomach. It had happened again. Another man had treated her like she was a piece of rag. She had just been another useless plaything that got annoying, so she got tossed into the rain on the side of the street, thrown away like a used coffee cup, like a dog.

Mary couldn't think of a single man who had treated her respectfully. Her father demanded respect every second and yet rarely, if ever, reciprocated it. All the boyfriends she had tentatively formed a relationship with ended up mistreating her. Before Mark and his *"extra-curricular dealings,"* there had been Sam. Gentle, sweet Sam—at least that's what Mary thought at first. He had dark brown hair and soft brown eyes, which were soulful and comical at the same time. They had been dating for a few months, sharing more and more of their lives with each other, until Sam met her father at the *Young and Promising Leaders* Fundraising Dinner, which Mary had invited him to. It was as though a different person came out of that day, and from then on, Sam had become disdainful of Mary, scathing of her ambitions, and less kind when she tried to speak of their future.

After a couple of weeks, Mary summoned the courage to ask Sam what had changed between them. She had told herself that the YPL event had been a coincidence and that something must have been amiss before then. Sam had turned those beautiful eyes on her and rested his hand on the back of hers. "Listen, I really admire your father, Mary."

His words seemed to pour cold water down her spine. Confused, she thought, *"This had something to do with her father, then."*

"We talked for a while that day. He might be tough, but I need him on my side. I have ambitions, Mary, and your father can help me. I don't want to do anything to upset him. He's a powerful man, and I admire him."

"But what does that have to do with us? Why have things been different since then?" Mary tried to hold his hand, but his grasp slipped away gently.

"I thought we might have a future, Mary, but your father enlightened me a little, I guess, about how you can't really drive yourself forward, that you are..." Sam looked away and pulled a face of clear distaste. "You're pretty needy, Mary, and I don't need that right now. I want to move forward with my life, and I don't have the capacity to handle your... issues."

Mary had looked at him, stunned. Her own father had done this, sabotaging what had been a perfectly happy relationship. Why though? Wasn't it enough that her father didn't really care about her? Did he have to stop everyone else from caring about her too? Or could it be that part of him wanted Mary kept away from romantic relationships with other people, as Grayson simply could not stand it if Mary's loyalty to him were shared even slightly? Mary wondered about the other possibility; she quickly quelled it. Her father didn't even realize that she knew what he had done, so he couldn't possibly be trying to protect his secret if he thought she didn't know it in the first place. Unprecedented hate swelled in Mary's heart. All Grayson Hart did was kill everything that threatened to bloom in his sight. She squeezed her eyes shut as images of that dreaded night from so long ago flashed in and out of her mind. "Murderer," she muttered under her breath. "Murderer," she said again, this time louder. Mary heaved a sigh as her lips quivered. Deep down in her heart, Mary knew she didn't hate her father. She could never really force herself to, and for that, her mother's lifeless eyes chased her day in and day out. The dilemma in her heart was as strong as the alcohol that coursed through her veins earlier, except that it was more bitter, coarse, and damaging. *"Elise, get up!"* The memory of those words breezed through her mind. Mary jammed her eyes shut again, shaking her head as though the thoughts would flee through her ears if she shook it hard enough.

Mary staggered in the rain, crying and occasionally letting out a small shout of outrage at her father, the cab driver, and the world. She caught her heel against a broken paving stone and fell forward, landing painfully on one knee. Ripping the too-high heels from her feet, she held them in one hand, dangling by the impractical straps. So, now barefoot, Mary approached the Murphyne Bridge. It loomed high into the darkened sky before her, stretching high across the swollen and aggressive river, a harsh and bold structure against the beauty of the water and nature-lined banks. The steel columns rose proudly from the water's depths and towered above her.

The street noise was much diminished now; fewer cars sped past, and the roar of the river replaced the traffic din. People were either where they would be for the evening or had decided to stay put and avoid the torrential rain. Her senses were still hazy from the intoxicating effects of the alcohol. Mary suddenly became aware of the vibration from her bag. Pulling out her phone, she squinted to focus on it. 7 missed calls and 10 text messages—an unprecedented amount. In fact, her phone hardly came this alive except after a test or exam, and her father was ready to eagle in on her. All of the attempts made to reach her by her stepmother and roommate. Angelica probably lost her key again and was out in the cold.

Mary stared at the messages and the missed calls, including one from her father. She thought that if she tried hard, she might feel remorse, but as it was, numbed by her misery and circumstances, she felt, with a clarity that was new to her, that she simply didn't want that old self back. Glancing up at the blackened road, she looked over to the other side of the bridge.

A car whizzed past, and Mary felt the light spray hit her face and body. She barely flinched.

"Should I cross over to the other side of the bridge?" Mary wondered. It suddenly seemed like an important question. *"Shall I remain Mary here or go to the other side and change things?"* Mary stayed with the thought, abstract as it was. *"I could become someone else. A different person. Someone with a different future than mine? I could care less about people's disapproval."* Mary imagined throwing her phone over the bridge and, with it, her old self, with all the pain and loneliness disappearing underneath the dark, cold water. *"That will end all the voices in my head."*

Silencing the vibration of her phone, Mary walked on. She could cross the bridge and be someone else on the other side of it. Forget the people who tried to reach her. Did Angelica want to borrow some money to tide her over until the end of the month? Did her father want to tell her how much harder she had to work and that she was letting him down? Her stepmother, who found it hard enough to keep her own emotions on track to worry about those of her husband's daughter, probably loved her but thought it too awkward to say it out loud. Mary felt a flash of strength course through her veins. In that split second, she could walk away from all of it.

A crack in the pavement caused Mary to trip, and as she failed to keep her balance, she fell again, not heavily but awkwardly enough to cause the contents of her bag to spill out onto the sidewalk. She dropped to her knees and began scrabbling around on the rain-slicked pavement, trying to gather her things together again, feeling weak and powerless; her moment of strength had left her. The tears that fell from her face were in sync with the raindrops that fell from the sky. The sky was crying with her too.

As she haphazardly tried to put everything back into her bag, a car came to a screeching halt by the road, and a man got out immediately and rushed over to where she still kneeled on the sidewalk. The car was a bright blue BMW, quite new, and the man, even though she couldn't see his face clearly, was handsome and had a look of genuine concern on his face. A spark lit inside her, and Mary was consumed by anger that another man—one who didn't even know her—was pretending to care about her and would probably end up doing something to hurt her. God, he could be a mugger for all she knew. Was he trying to take advantage of a young woman in trouble? Did he go around in his car looking for vulnerable girls to hurt?

The spark turned into flames, and Mary yelled, "Leave me alone! Don't you dare touch me!" The man jumped back in surprise. He was wearing a suit that was getting wet, and somehow, she realized he didn't fit with her idea that he was trying to mug her, or worse, but her anger was too consuming for her to believe he was trying to help.

The man held out his hands, palms facing forward, in the classic "it's okay, I'm backing off" gesture, and he spoke deliberately, kindly, and gently to Mary. "I saw you in the rain; I saw you fall while I was driving, and I wondered if you needed help, that's all." He pointed to her feet. "You have no shoes on, and I thought you might use some help; that was all. Are you okay?"

Mary almost roared at him, such was her rising hysteria and rage. "Leave me alone! Leave me alone! I don't need you. I don't need anyone!" She watched, bristling with anger, as the man backed away from her, his hands still expressing his attempt to calm her, and then broke into a hasty walk back into the comfort and dry haven of his car. He slammed the door and sped off as though he was in a hurry to get somewhere, which made his gesture of stopping for her even more unlikely. Mary started to think he might have been one of the good ones, but what did it matter? He was gone, like everyone else. Granted, she had scared him off, but alas, he wasn't here anyway.

She scrambled to her feet, which were now crying out against the cold and dirt. She was cold and wet from standing in the rain. She sniffled as she clutched her bag closer to her body, the shoes hanging from one hand. Mary looked down the road across the bridge and thought she could see something, but the rain and the dim light made it difficult to focus.

She waited for the rear lights and headlights of the cars to go past and let her eyes adjust a little. "No, I must be seeing things. This can't be happening." In a single moment, every aspect of the night fell away from Mary. There was only this moment and the horror ahead of her. With every ounce of strength and every nerve straining to join in the effort, she screamed with more passion and desperation than she knew she possessed. "What are you doing? Someone Help! Stop!" Mary's heart started to thunder in her ears as she threw herself onto the road, her feet slamming against the hard road. *Right. Left. Right. Left. Right.* What she was looking at was enough to jolt all traces of alcohol out of her system. Mary picked up the pace as she yelled again. "NO! Stop!" *Left. Right. Left. Right.* She had to stop it. She had to make it in time.

12
THE SIGNS

Like the feathery kiss of a ghost that never was,
The future beckons,
Telling secrets of the past and hereafter

The rain was lashing down now, heavier than it had just moments ago, hitting the pavement so hard that the water was flying upwards in a violent rebound. The sound was an insistent drumbeat, sped up many times as though to match this very moment. The sky was unnaturally dark, and people hurried left and right for shelter. The forecast, delivered by that cheerful weatherman John Murphy, had been for a pleasant and gentle evening, so this deluge was unexpected. John couldn't help but think how weathermen got paid so much money yet made mistakes so often. It didn't seem right that they got rich while messing up so much. But what did he know?

John was wondering, but not for the same reason as everyone else. As he kept up a determined stride towards the Murphyne Bridge, he allowed his mind to wander back to the days when he had communicated his dreams and aspirations to

God and to his most recent anguish that he had been abandoned to his misery. Although John had never been deeply religious, he, like many people, carried a degree of spirituality with him, and he had prayed as best he could.

Could this unprecedented downpour, the thunder, and the lightning be a sign for him? It did seem as though, with every step John took, the rain drove harder, glancing off every surface, and the lightning and thunder took over the skies with such dramatic effect. Was this God telling him to stop? John snorted. He couldn't stop now.

Enjoying the relative quietness of the streets now that the fierce weather had driven most people away to find shelter and turning over in his mind these thoughts about God and signs, John recalled the parable of the lost sheep, which was taught at Sunday School. He remembered the story that if a shepherd had one hundred sheep and one went astray, he would leave the ninety-nine sheep on the hillside to search for the stray animal. When he finds the sheep that had strayed, his heart is filled with joy at the returning sheep, with even more rejoicing than at the ninety-nine sheep that did not stray.

Was John a stray sheep that God wanted to bring home? Could the storm be a sign that God's eye and guiding hand were upon him? The thought that he was worthy of God's love and that that love was strong enough to try to prevent John from carrying out his plan was powerful.

A light, not a strong one, but a small, weak flicker, seemed to come on in that black hole that ate into John's mind. Was there hope? John turned around and stared back down the street where he had just walked. He drew both hands to his face to wipe the rainwater away from his eyes and pull back the rain-slicked hair to his forehead. All that he knew was back down that way, and he was walking further away from it.

He looked down along the street and then ahead of him, towards the bridge. It stood before him like a beacon in the fog. The rain obscured his vision but not his feelings.

He allowed himself to think for one moment about walking back home, reaching the front door, and walking back into the embrace of his family. The lights glowing, and the coat rack full. His mother and brothers would be distraught at his disappearance and note, and the sight of him returning would surely give them some relief or even make them envelop him in their love. He closed his eyes as he imagined his mother's warm, soft arms surrounding him, comforting him, like when he was a child. His brothers would think about how they treated him over the years, and finally, he would have a sense of belonging—even though the love came at the expense of his life.

As John stood there with his eyes closed and himself fully encompassed in this imaginative event, he felt a big smile start to grow on his face.

The flicker of light inside John suddenly pulsed brighter, and he felt the possibility of the future. Before, he had thought there was no alternative for him, and now he was surprised by how tightly he wanted to hold on to that glimmer of hope.

John rubbed his face in the rain, as if washing it, and let the droplets cleanse him. He smiled at the gray sky, fanning the flame of hope within himself. He looked back towards the bridge again, gave a smiling, rueful small shake of his head, and turned to walk back home. He knew that, from all the signs, he shouldn't do what he was about to do. Maybe his life could be better.

At that moment, a car came speeding towards him with its headlights almost blinding John's eyes, traveling not only over the speed limit but incredibly dangerously, considering the risk of aquaplaning on the wet road. John caught his breath and braced himself to leap left or right, depending on whether the driver kept control of the speeding vehicle. The car somehow gripped the road, and the driver appeared to accelerate slightly as it passed John. The wheels plowed through a deep puddle by the side of the road, just where John stood. A sheet of dirty water sprayed over him as the car went past. John froze, and without even realizing it, a harsh laugh escaped from his mouth as he spat out the filthy water that had splashed in his mouth and watched the car hurry on like nothing had happened. *Au contraire,* something *had* happened.

Of course, John was already wet from the rain, and the water from the car hardly made him wetter, but it wasn't the degree of wetness in his hair or clothes that bothered him. It was the message in the water. Right then and there, as John spat out the sandy water, he knew that there was no going back for him: no second-guessing, no changing his mind. It was as though the water had very literally washed all hope away. John's resolve hardened and sprouted more anger inside him, enough to drive his determination even harder.

John stared at the back of the car as it continued its manic pace down the bridge. It was a vibrant and familiar shade of blue that stood out even in the dark, and he could hardly see the license plate or the person driving the car so recklessly. For a moment, John thought the car looked familiar, but he quickly cast his mind to other pressing issues, like his current dilemma.

He had turned towards home, but fate had intervened and warned him off. His heart, a sinking stone in his chest, looked sadly towards his homeward route, this time knowing he would not change his mind again. He gazed at it for a few moments, the welcoming images of his mother and brothers dissolving like chalk drawings in the rain.

As John gazed toward home, he seemed to gaze clearly at his past. Memories struck him like the raindrops on his body, and they seemed to form a collage of all the events that led him here. He could imagine snapshots of those moments and events; he saw them lined up together, almost like inspirations on a college girl's fashion mood board. But there was nothing positive in them. They were all of the small, seemingly insignificant events that had eventually linked together to form a chain that had pulled him through the years of his life, through the last few difficult months, to this place and this moment.

Memory after memory, John sifted through his past, eventually settling on one particularly disturbing one. He recalled it as one of the moments when he felt ashamed to be himself and so alone. He had been learning to play the guitar at school, and the group had planned a recital for assembly one morning. John knew he wasn't very good, at least not as good as the other kids in the group, but he enjoyed it, and no one gave him a hard time. He simply existed in the group not to even make friends, as he had been so desperate to, but to simply have that one thing he enjoyed all to himself. The innocence of that desire to have a special hobby was soon tarnished and dragged through the proverbial mud. However, the other boys and girls in the group had decided on a plan: when the music reached the final movement, the group—except for John—would suddenly stop playing, which was a plot to humiliate him.

The group played the first piece, and it all went well. Then, as the second and final piece was coming to a close and John was really engrossed in it, the guitars around him suddenly fell silent, and the twanging, unpleasant, and out-of-tune noise he was making echoed around the hall. There was a moment of silence, and then the whole school seemed to erupt with laughter. John's face heated up very quickly, with blood rushing in his ears as he became flustered and hot tears of humiliation burning their trail down his cheeks. He hadn't played the guitar since the horrible event.

He recalled another moment when he was just a young man and life was somewhat positive and not so unbearable. His family had been out for a rare day out in a neighboring town, and they were sitting together; his parents were feasting on a bowl of ice cream, and John and his brothers were eating chips and candy. The sun was starting its descent, and a warm glow in the late afternoon seemed to lull everyone into a pleasant suspension of normal activity. Families and couples around them seemed equally reluctant to pack up their bags and pile everyone into cars and strollers for the journey home.

John had felt hugged by the light and the soft air. He saw his parents exchange what John thought were contented looks. Given the events that followed, John figured he must have thought wrong. His mom and dad seemed to fight around the clock about everything. The house never seemed peaceful. However, this particular afternoon was very different; in fact, it was undeniably so. Maybe that afternoon, they'd just run out of energy for it. But at this moment, it was calm. His brothers were playing good-naturedly. Nothing could go wrong. When they all finally trouped back to the car, arms slung around each other's shoulders, bags swinging from hands, John felt peaceful, sleepy, and happy. He felt pure, deep happiness that warmed his skin and heart.

The next morning, what had seemed like the onset of something beautiful became sour in their mouths. It was like dark, thick, pregnant clouds replaced the warm sunny atmosphere with darkness and ominous threats of an unforgiving downpour. Everyone except John's father slept late. The father of three had woken up early and put on the same clothes he wore the day before, with a sinister deed in his heart. Without much care or remorse, the man took the contents of the emergency fund jar, leaving it as empty as his black, unfeeling heart, and took the train wherever he thought his new life might be waiting for him. He had taken the time to fling a few clothes and his tub of shaving cream in a bag, but he hadn't left a note. He didn't leave anything except the unbearable taste of bitterness in the mouths of those he once called family.

"At least I left a note. Everyone will know why I ended up here. I want them to know. I don't want to leave a mystery."

More memories rushed out of their dark hiding place, some fragmented, some as powerful as a fist to the jaw. John was going through all these memories like one would a scrapbook. He was slowly acknowledging that he was coming to the end of his short life, and the innate prompt to look back on it all was hard to ignore or even fight.

The parent-teacher conferences that no one attended. The time he got a speaking part in a play at school, he rehearsed tirelessly so that his parents would be so proud of him. It was a small part consisting of him being a corrupt businessman who was up to no good, and it was his job to be menacing yet kind-hearted in equal measure. John had stood in the wings, gripping the edges of his character's brown felt hat, waiting to go out into those dazzling lights and deliver his lines brilliantly.

THE SIGNS

The moment finally came. John had gone out, clomping in his "Bad Guy" boots, and while he held his position on stage, he took a moment to glance towards the seats where his family was sitting. He wouldn't sabotage the play by doing anything unprofessional, like waving or anything, but he might give Sean a slight wink. As his eyes became accustomed to the bright stage lights and the darkness of the auditorium, even though it was slightly difficult to see, John saw the row of seats, which he had proudly booked for his whole family, standing empty. The program for the show was lying neatly where it had been placed, on each seat. His family wasn't there. They hadn't come to see him after all.

John felt hot tears rush to his eyes, and he blinked furiously to keep them from spilling down his face. He forgot two lines, delivered the others without conviction, and left the theater all by himself. He had imagined that his family would meet him at the stage door, and they might all go for a milkshake or something on the way home. John walked a mile home and arrived home to find that his mother had gone out to cover an extra shift at work, and his brothers had found better things to do—video games and arguing about girls. The tickets to the show were still on the table by the mailbox, where they'd always been.

John picked them up, tore them into pieces, and threw them into the kitchen trash can. He never mentioned the show to his mother that night, and she never said a word either. Had she forgotten? Or did she not care? Who knows? It's too late now, anyway. *"Water under the bridge,"* thought John grimly.

As these thoughts bombarded him, John began to walk slowly toward the bridge. He felt as though everyone around him was being sped up, like fast-forwarding a film, and rushing past him in the rain, seeking shelter. It seemed that only he was moving at a normal pace toward the destiny that was his.

"Destiny," he thought, *"is a curious thing."* It is, by definition, the endgame, the thing that awaits us. Why do we bother to fight it? Why do people attempt to change it? *"What is my endgame? What do I do to cope with all this while I wait for it? Why is my life like this?"* It seemed so cruel. It seemed so unfair. Why couldn't the fates have smiled on him a little more? What had he done to deserve this? What had he done to feel this way?

John came to the bridge. He glanced down at the graffiti-lined crags that lined the river before giving way to vivid green trees and vegetation along the riverbanks. Treacherous mud framed the banks, which the river failed to consume despite the heavy rain. He took a minute to compose himself, taking in the drop of water for the first time, feeling slightly dizzy. Staring down from the heights of the bridge, he felt a sense of power over his life that had long since been out of reach. In these next moments, he would decide his fate. He would control the outcome of what would happen next. The spray-painted letters glared at him in luminous colors from the granite rocks. Climbers had clung perilously to those rocks to share their messages with drivers leaving the town; messages of passion for their causes or remembrance of loved ones shone from the rocks. Did John have a cause? No, that had slipped through his fingertips with each rejection letter. He had played this scene in his mind countless times. John was about to leave his own message—that he would decide what came next and show them he was capable of strength. He placed his hands upon the cold, heavy handrail, first his right hand, then his left. *This is it.* John's thoughts had a clarity that he hadn't known before.

Each word and each syllable seemed to be cut from crystal. The unspoken words seemed to carve a place in the air before him. *This is it.*

He was aware of cars rushing by on the bridge. The universe wasn't going to stop revolving—not for him or anyone. A group of people dashed by, seeking shelter from the rain, oblivious to what was happening so close to them. John knew that he was just a guy. A guy on the bridge. His backpack was like any other backpack. His appearance was so unremarkable, he might as well be invisible. If anyone had glanced at his face, though, regardless of his lack of physical appeal, they would have noticed the sheen of tears on his face. Even then, they would probably think that he had broken up with his girlfriend or something equally mundane, and that he would cry and move on.

Just then, a car went past at a slightly slower speed than the others. In the car were two young men and two ladies, each probably between 19 and 22 years old. They seemed to be returning from a wild party. The driver had one of the girls on the passenger side, and they were both jamming to the music from the radio. The other two in the back were drunk to a stupor and acting all cozy in the back seat until they sighted the young man at the bridge. They screamed through their cords, "Do it! Jump! Jump, dude!" to gales of laughter from inside the car. It was a small thing, but it made John realize how needlessly and pointlessly cruel people could be.

John's chin dropped to his chest in a confused, desperate sadness and shame. He gripped the handrail so tightly that the underside of his hand paled and the veins popped. *This is it, then. It's over. It's done. No more pain. The size of the bridge's structure, so imposing and significant on the landscape, felt like it was naturally the place where John could bring a conclusion to his anguish. With the bridge being such a prominent part of the town and the lifeline to moving freely to other places, there was perhaps a beautiful irony in this place being where John could move to freedom.* There was nothing left in him. He couldn't fight the rising tide of sadness and depression any longer. The oily blackness inside him had won. He was only seventeen. He'd had enough of misery and anger. He didn't want to cry himself to sleep anymore. He didn't want another single morning of waking to this life. He didn't want to encounter any more cruel people like the ones in that car. He just wanted peace, far away from all the chaos. He could stop it all right now, right here.

John threw back his head, eyes wide open, hands grasping the icy metal of the bridge, ready to embrace his fate. His shaking legs climbed over the hefty rail as his hands latched on to it for support. The flashing warning lights illuminated the tear tracks on his cheeks as he steadied himself, staring into the rushing water below. The process was slow and tedious, and the thunder drowned out John's raggedy breathing.

Soon, he was teetering on the edge of the rail, and there was no barrier between him and his harsh fate anymore. Even from high above, where he balanced precariously in the dim light of the storm, he could see perilous currents and jagged rocks below. His fingers weakly clung to the rail behind him as he looked down at his imminent end. "No more!" he screamed to the sky. "No more. It's over!" He prepared himself to launch into peace—to end all the voices he heard in his head—and into the end of his life. To end the nightmare that he was living. John held his breath and got ready.

13

LEAVING IT ALL BEHIND

A tear-stained face like the stained glass
Of the ethereal cathedral of sadness,
I pick myself up, leaving the pain behind

Mary's scream was whisked away by the wind. Her hair was plastered to her face by the rain, and every tendon and muscle in her body felt taut and strained. "No!" Another cry was taken by the wind that blew in from the ocean. "Don't. Please don't do it." Suddenly, Mary ran, her bare feet slapping against the wet pavement. Was he really doing what she thought? Could this really be happening? Mary was terrified, and even though she ran toward him, she felt hopelessly inadequate. What could she, a hurting soul, do to help this other hurting soul? And yet, some small part of her also felt electrifyingly alive.

As she ran, she whisked past what looked like a couple. How do they not see this? Cars were rushing past the bridge, and Mary was shocked at how they could just drive past. Surely the drivers and passengers could see him? How could they just drive past? Is it just her? Has she lost her mind, and was she just imagining this?

The boy on the bridge was leaning forward, staring intently at the black, swirling water below. Mary could see that his center of gravity was almost certainly at a tipping point, and if he leaned just a little further, if the wind blew hard down the bridge, if he lost his footing on the wet pavement for a second... the thought was too horrifying.

And still, cars drove by, ignoring the boy on the bridge. Were all the drivers too distracted by the rain or by the oncoming headlights? Were the passengers too worried about getting home in time for dinner? Whether they'd remember to buy a bag of groceries? Had they left that file on their desk? And in the meantime, this desperate young man clung to the bridge, leaning forward, as though he had made up his mind about something but was, for these moments, teetering between his two possible fates.

And Mary ran. She was vaguely aware of sharp things digging into her feet as she sped along the pavement, the rain blurring her vision. The alcohol in her system was still softening the edges of reality, but now it was also affording her clarity and energy that she hadn't known before. All the while, she yelled. She wanted him to hear her, to just look around for a second, to give her enough time to reach him before... Mary shook the thought from her mind and kept running. "Stop! Stop, please!" She was near enough now to see that the boy's eyes were shut. He hadn't been staring at the water after all.

Mary knew she was close enough now for him to hear her, but he didn't respond. Dirty water from the puddles at the side of the road sprayed Mary every time a car went by, but she couldn't have cared less. "Stop it! No way. Don't do this. Stop!'" Her voice fought the wind, the pounding rain, and the sound of the traffic roaring by. As she neared him, Mary felt as though all of those things—the night, the weather, the people in the cars—weren't real, or at least that they belonged to a different reality. The only solid things in the world at that very moment were Mary, the boy, and the bridge.

She felt powerful and light, as though all the sadness, anger, and hopelessness were being shed as she ran. They were insubstantial now. She could leave them behind. An energy had rushed in and filled that space where the pain in her life had been. She needed that energy to reach him. In a rush, she remembered what the cab driver had said to her: "Find someone to take care of, lady." How prophetic those words had been!

The figure on the bridge seemed to lurch forward a little, and Mary screamed into the driving rain. She wasn't going to reach him in time; she wasn't going to make it. Her scream cutting through the night, Mary made a desperate leap toward the boy...

~

John stood with his hands resting on the handrail. It felt solid and cold beneath his hands. He felt the rain on his face, but not just wetness as a whole. He could feel each raindrop on his skin. The lines between reality and this moment were blurred. John felt as though the rain was making itself known to him, as though each raindrop wanted to find him. It was a curious feeling. John felt embraced by the rain, as though he were one with something greater than himself—benevolent yet comforting. With a ripple of understanding that warmed every part of his being, John realized that he felt peaceful.

"This is what it takes, huh?" John thought to himself, the bitter humor of the situation not escaping him. He couldn't hear the traffic blaring past him. He couldn't feel the increasing chill of the wind. There was just him and the soft, welcome patter of the raindrops on his body. It was almost euphoric. Oh, that feeling of peace was like a restoration of his entire spirit. John had never been in love, but he imagined there, at that moment, that love had to feel like this.

The girls he liked barely knew he existed. Even if one of them had shown any interest, John would have backed away. He didn't have the confidence to get close to a girl, so the world of mutual love for another, kissing a beloved with affection, was strange to him.

But it didn't matter now. He had this glorious moment. Everything was in its place; everything was as it should be. That meant John felt quite sure he was doing the right thing. How else would he know this *peace*? It had to be right.

His short life had contained more pain, worry, and sadness than he had been able to carry. This was the first night he could remember that it didn't arrive, accompanied by panic and fear about what the morning would bring. There was just this night, and it was wonderful.

There was no noise of worry, confusion, or dissatisfaction in his head. John felt as though some great source of anguish, whatever it was that had blighted the last few years of his life, had been switched off.

"This is the greatest moment of my life," thought John. He had never felt like he fit into whatever time and place he was

in. This time, at this moment, in this place, he was exactly where he needed to be; he fit right in.

John tilted his head back, enjoying the rain touching him and soothing him even more. He felt a great power drawn from being in this place, about to embrace his fate. *Never again, no more pain. He was leaving it all behind.*

"I don't belong here. I never belonged here." And yet, there was something all of a sudden—the briefest stutter of hesitation, a moment of confusion. John dismissed it. Better confusion than the constant hurt, the shadow, that welled inside him for so long. If he failed now, he knew life would become harder. This beautiful, safe, soft moment was his and his alone. It had always been waiting for him, and now he greeted it like a lover, like an embrace he'd always known would come. *"It's time. It's time. I can go now; I can go."* In this ethereal, abstract moment, somehow, John's physical nature submitted, and he took a deep breath into his lungs, his hands releasing their grip on the handrail. John let go of the railing and felt the light as he began to fall. His upper body slid, tilted, and started to descend; he felt the air rush past his ears. Every single cell of his body awakened and was poised to drink in this wonderful event.

He felt surrounded by air; he felt light, weightless, and suspended. He felt like Superman, his boyhood hero. Superman was a stranger in a different land, never able to fully become part of his environment. He, too, lacked a crowd of friends and was known as a geek—a nerd.

John had long identified with the ultimate hero, who had to hide his powers behind the lonely, singular geek whom nobody noticed. In his bedroom, long into the night, or during moments spent daydreaming on the bus home, John would imagine a world where he was a superhero and be forced to pretend to be this lonely, introverted, tortured boy. If only John could commit an act of ultimate bravery to save the world and then unmask himself to everyone, he would be loved and admired by men and women alike. His mother would be proud of him, and his brothers would be jealous.

And so, John fell, his eyes already closed, a superhero at last. This act, in itself, unmasked him as who he really was at last. He was saving himself, even if he couldn't save anyone else. Even behind his eyelids, John saw grayness as he finally let go and waited for freedom, for the light to emerge. The elements around him had melted away; he felt the rush of air cleansing his worries. The act of letting go had liberated him beyond any worry that had been plaguing him. He felt one hundred emotions at once, and they were euphoric; nothing mattered; he was free. The air was racing past him; that split second of letting go had released him from his ties.

"What would happen? Has it happened?" John wondered, unwilling to open his eyes and see for himself. Would an angel suddenly appear with arms outstretched to welcome him? As he continued to fall, waiting for it all to end, John could hear a ringing noise in his ears, and he struggled to figure out what it was.

14
I AM NOT ALONE

Hope springs
From a patch of soil
In a barren field of thorns
I know now that I am not alone

John tried to gather his thoughts and organize them into something familiar. Something wasn't right. Edges of dark reality began to creep in, like paint dripping into clear water, blossoming in the blissful world he had inhabited a moment ago. He could feel something solid. He realized that his skin felt cold and clammy. The soft, dreamlike state fell away from him, and he frowned as though concentrating on something beyond his understanding. "This isn't right. I'm still here, on the bridge."

John lay there in shock, with his eyes still jammed shut. His squeezed eyelids got even tighter as a heavy drop of rain struck them. Something jerked his body. *"Is God playing a trick on me?"* John thought hazily as he felt pressure around his waist again. His mind and thoughts were clouded as he tried to decipher what was happening. His hands flailed, and, to his horror, he caught hold of the handrail again. He was still on the bridge. He felt as though he was emerging from an anesthetic, as though he were swimming upwards from the bottom of a swimming pool. Gradually, his senses started to accept the reality of the world around him.

The blissful, hypnotic moment was leaving him. He suddenly heard sounds—cars swinging past, voices somewhere. He didn't want to, but against his will, his eyes opened and confirmed his horror. He was still on the bridge. He hadn't fallen. Something was pulling at him, clawing at him, holding him.

The last protective lenses separating him from the world fell away as he involuntarily turned around. He saw a woman; her face was contorted with fear and anguish. She was screaming at him, "No, no. Please no. Don't do this. Please stop, for the love of God, stop!"

~

Mary had leaped toward the boy on the bridge like an athlete who had spent years training for this moment. She didn't have time to think about how she would do it or what she should say. She just grabbed him, feeling, even as she did so, the momentum of his body moving forward. She had caught him at exactly the very last split second available. A fraction later would have been too late, and she would not have been able to save him—or herself.

Mary wasn't able to stop her screams. She clung so hard to the young man as though he were trying to free himself from her when, in fact, the shock had caused him to go limp in her arms. It was as though he had no fight in him, and although he looked physically strong and had a much larger build than her, his weakened state meant that she could maintain a grip on him. She carried on screaming and clutching him to her, terrified of stopping. Mary felt that if she released her grip on this young man, she would be a failure at everything, forever. Mary tightened her grip around his waist as though she were holding onto herself. Every muscle in her arms ached with the effort, but Mary was determined not to let go of this boy, not for anything.

Some part of her knew she saw herself in this young man, and as she chanted, "I won't let go," she knew she was speaking to both the boy and herself. Right then and there, Mary was holding on to many things: herself, Mary Hart, and her freedom from the pain and anguish caused by her mother's death at her father's hands. She didn't need to dress like this to change. She didn't need to be anyone else. She could somehow be herself. If only she could hold on to this boy, then she could hold on to herself. She felt that if she let him go, she would have let herself go forever. Joe Sampson's words came to her again. *Find someone to take care of, pretty lady."* How right he had been! This was her someone. This young man, who had given up just like her, was the someone she needed to truly see herself.

Mary saw with a jolt of horror that the boy's eyes were closing again, and she wondered in a panic if he was falling unconscious. Her grip slipped slightly, and she said out loud, "I will not let go of you." She felt as though she held the fate of the universe in her embrace, as though, for that moment, she was the caretaker of humanity. If she could succeed at saving this young man's life, then the world would be a better place for it. Mary reveled in her regret, wondering if things would have turned out differently if she had just walked into the room that night. Perhaps her mother would not have met that dark, undeserved fate. She imagined that she had walked into the room that night and held Grayson Hart back, the way she held this stranger, before Grayson shoved her mother to an untimely end that night. She imagined that this was how she saved her mother.

She became aware of her skinny arms and weak upper body and cursed that she'd given up all the sports at school at which she had excelled to give in to the pressure of schoolwork and her responsibilities. But then she felt a primal roar within her build into a surge of power that escaped her lips and renewed her grip at the same time. With that deep, human cry charging out from her small body, Mary pulled the boy back against the railing. With monumental effort and a loud, lioness-like yell, Mary began to heave at his body, trying to drag him back over the railing. She closed her eyes in a silent moment of thanks for the rain, as the slick wetness made it easier to slide the boy over the railing, despite his weight. He slumped backward heavily, her lioness's strength pulling them both to the ground. The boy lay directly on top of Mary, his body limp and his breath hot and stale. They lay still on the sidewalk, stunned and confused, for different reasons. Mary didn't flinch when a raindrop from his face dropped right into her left eye. She wouldn't let herself flinch at this moment. The rain hammered down on them, the night slunk around them, and the girl clung to the young man still, even though they were now collapsed on the sidewalk and the young man showed no signs of struggling.

The boy looked at her, his eyes clearing yet wearing a mask of confusion and something else she couldn't quite decipher. He collapsed beside her. Mary sat up, staring at him, her body wracked with strain from what she had just done, soaking wet and barefoot, her face communicating everything she felt better than words could express. The concern on her face was unmistakable, and it was all for this boy.

~

John tried to pull his mind into some kind of order to allow him some understanding of the chain of events that had just occurred. It was so hard. His mind seemed to want to slip away from what had happened, and John felt faint. He could feel the cold of the rain-slicked sidewalk beneath him, and he was content for the moment to remain there.

Gradually, his mind started to clear. He began to see the dampness of his clothes and the position of his body on the sidewalk, and he began to put together the pieces of the puzzle. Mary saw him glancing at his palms, which had recently gripped the edge of the bridge. He stretched his fingers awkwardly, like he had only just realized that he had fingers at all. With a look of shock and confusion plastered on his face, John replayed the hazy memory of what had just happened in his mind. He tried to make sense of it all. The memories were blurry and hardly decipherable as he slowly recalled the moment that he had let go. He remembered how his fingers slowly slid away from his cold grip on the railing. And yet here he was. The clouds began to clear in his mind, and a tear slipped from his eyes. As Mary watched it slide down his cheek, something happened. The shadow, which had wreaked so much sadness and despair in his life, seemed to melt into tears, and those tears rushed through him like a tidal wave of grief. Grief for himself, the boy who was almost lost to the world, for the young man who had no future, no hope. The tears kept pouring, accompanied by sobs that shook his body. And the young woman, this girl who came out of the rain-lashed night to save him, held him close and absorbed each of his wracking cries into her slight body.

Mary held him tight, squeezing her eyes closed as she felt his sadness flow from him in howling sobs. His sadness and unrestrained emotion poured from him as immense cries jolted through him. Mary didn't waver; she kept holding him, not letting him feel for one second like he was alone in this.

Eventually, the boy's great sobs became less intense. Mary clung to him tightly; she didn't want any space between them. She needed him to know that she had him and that he was safe. Her grip didn't falter. She cried too, although she wasn't sure for whom. She cried for both of them, in truth: for this lost boy, with such despair and sadness in his soul, and for herself. *"Find somebody to take care of, lady."* And she had. Mary held this stranger, whose raw emotions poured from him, and she held him tight. The world was going on beyond the Murphyne Bridge, but right now, two souls had found each other, and it was a moment as great as any in the world. *"I am not alone,"* thought Mary. *"None of us are."*

15

REALIZATION

Like a rude awakening,
The epiphany settles thick and heavy

Mary wasn't sure how long they sat motionless. The young man half-sat, half-laid across her lap, while her arms encircled him. There was something maternal about how she held him and how he lay heavy and trusting in her embrace. As the hour grew later, the traffic heading across the bridge became less frequent. Mary could see faces peering at them through the darkness and rain, speeding past. The faces were blurred images of superficial concern and confusion. What did they look like? A young man and woman, wet and disheveled, one barefoot, comforting each other, sat beneath the soaring supports in the rain on Murphyne Bridge. Maybe they looked like they'd been partying and had run out of booze, energy, or both.

His sobs, heavy and jolting, continuously shook his body. The boy's breath came in rasping gasps between bouts of tears. Mary sensed that years of torment were pouring forth from him. From time to time, he moaned as though recalling a terrible, heartbreaking event, and then his cries would begin afresh. There seemed to be little to say; it was only important that she held him and was there for him. An understanding seemed to blossom in Mary—that she had to hold on to this boy. Whatever it was that had brought him to this terrible point in his young life, he was here now. It was of the utmost importance that she stayed and held him and let him know she was there for him, no matter what.

The rain was starting to abate, and although there was still a regular drum of raindrops on the pavement, the heaviest of the downpour was over. Mary let herself think back over those times when she, too, had thought she had been ready to end it all. Carrying the weight of her father's terrible mistake and her mother's traumatizing death had always pulled her down so much that many times, she had thought, "What if..."

Had she ever really been close to taking her own life? Yes, she had thought about it, but she was too aware that she had much living to do. She knew that her mother would never want her to give up. That incredible woman who encouraged her to get up after falling on the playground would never want her to give up. Thinking of that distant memory, darkness clouded her mind at the reminder of what her father did. It was then that Mary realized she wanted to achieve things—not for her father or anyone else and their expectations, but for herself. Mary knew that she had many advantages that so many other people would give so much for, and she had plunged into a self-destructive cycle over her father, guys that treated her terribly, and worries about things that she could set right.

But this poor boy? How much had he been through to push him to this point? The harder he cried, the more resolute Mary felt about facing her own demons and facing them down. She didn't have to be a victim; she could see that now. It had taken this encounter to help her see how much she really had in her life. Mary's heart hurt, but no longer for herself but for this young man and whatever had driven him to this bridge. She felt tears prick at her eyelids as she wondered about the world and how much pain was being endured at any given moment. How could one small person make a difference? And yet, tonight, she had been given a chance to make a difference. Had she? Did she really help him? This boy in her arms could be an amazing person with so much to give.

John clung to the woman, unashamed and unable to stem the tears. Mary held him without flinching once. She barely shifted, even though she was uncomfortable, sitting on the cold pavement in barely any clothes and no shoes. She just held him. His spirit felt great torment. It had almost become too much. He had almost wanted to end it all for good and nearly succeeded. From deep within him, the years of conflict and unhappiness rose to the surface. But there was some part of it, for the first time, that felt okay. Not great, but just tentatively okay, that all of these emotions were finally pouring out of him. They were still at the edge of the bridge, barely out of harm's way, but neither of them could find the fortitude to move either way.

Mary saw the flash of the vehicle at a distance, and her heart sank. *"The company that I called earlier... the driver who kicked me out,"* she thought, with shame briefly coursing through her. She raised her eyes to see Joe Sampson, the cab driver.

Joe left, thinking she was a hopeless case. He left, thinking she wasn't worth the effort. Besides their unfortunate encounter, Joe was still not quite done for the night.

133

Not long after he left, he got a call for someone else who needed a ride. He was about to accept the job when Mary's face, covered with makeup and tears came into his mind. Her pathetic threats against him and her desperate loneliness which she projected without knowing, were completely unexplainable.

How could Joe have just dropped her out of the cab like that? His sense of guilt took over him as he stared at his phone screen, looking at the text message the operator sent him with the details of his intended passenger. Why would he just drop off a girl in the middle of the road and in the rain? She was also drunk.

He could never live with himself if anything happened to her. He thought about his daughter and her silly smile and then her sad face when she didn't have something she wanted. He couldn't imagine losing her—he couldn't imagine leaving her alone on a bridge, cold and in despair. If it were his daughter who was going through such a difficult time, he would not want the same thing done to her. He knew what he had to do now; it was all clear to him. After thinking intensely, Joe climbed back into his cab and began to search the empty streets for the girl. It didn't take long to get to Murphyne Bridge, and he heard the young lady screaming. He quickly parked on the side of the bridge, leaving his lights on so that he could see.

Joe's breathing picked up as his eyes widened at what they saw. Although terrifying, the sight of the two people clinging to each other at the very edge of that bridge was moving beyond belief under the strain of the storm. He saw a boy holding on to the young lady from the cab for his dear life. When Joe arrived at the scene, he could immediately sense the pain and despair that permeated the air around these two.

Joe stood there, catching his breath, watching them shift into a sitting position. Mary sat up and cradled the boy's head in her arms. Joe wondered what God had in mind for these two lost souls. With a sense of empathy and worry, he asked, "Can I help you two?" His voice was kind and low. These kids were in trouble, but not the kind that needed the police. Joe thought he had never seen two souls look more lost. He wondered what he could do to help them.

Mary, stopping to gather herself, stuttered an explanation of the evening's events. The dark look in her eye told him that the night had been horrendous, and as she spoke, he noticed the fear shaking her voice as she spoke of how she almost witnessed the boy taking his life. The ranting continued as she relived those moments through her words, and then it stopped. They remained there looking at each other as Mary took shaky, raggedy breaths, and then she told Joe in a tired voice that she was angry with him for ditching her out of his cab like that. "I know why you did it. Part of me doesn't blame you, but you shouldn't have done it! I was so scared. I'm still scared." Mary wasn't yelling; she didn't even have the strength to do that, but Joe understood everything.

He nodded, admonished but still marveling at her intrepid sense of entitlement. And yet, he realized privately, it had been the act of turning Mary out into the night that had brought her to this grief-stricken young man in his moment of absolute need. Everything does happen for a reason. But his thoughts about that could wait. The same thing would dawn on the girl later, he decided, and he smiled calmly.

Helping the two young people from their huddled position on the pavement, Joe walked them over to his cab. Mary looked again at the flash on the side of the car. *YHPRUM Cab*

Co. Mary did a double-take. *"Can that be right? I mean, I know I'd been drinking, and I was so upset, but I'm sure the company was Murphy Cabs."*

Shaking her head gently as though to clear her thoughts, Mary climbed into the back of the cab with the boy. He still clung to her like she was an amulet for good luck and protection. She sensed his shock and horror at what he had almost done. She had never felt like she was starved for attention before until she felt someone hug her like that. It was tighter than a normal hug. With that kind of hug, you find that you don't really want to let go. It was a good match for her disbelief at what had just happened that evening. Everyone in the cab fell into their own silence to reflect on the enormity of the events that had unfolded and lay between them. Mary leaned forward slightly to speak to the driver. "I want to make sure he gets home first. Is that okay?" She aimed the question at John, who nodded and murmured his home address to Joe. It didn't seem right to let him go alone, and Mary had no intention of letting this boy down.

Mary half-closed her eyes and stared at the night through the window as the car started and the journey to John's home began. The weather was starting to clear, as though the storm was happening within them. All the darkness seemed to disappear. One moment the world was drowned with thunder rumbling in the distance; the next, the sky was shot through with moonlight, and the rain clouds were letting up and moving on. *"How like life that is,"* thought Mary. *"I was ready to put myself on a horrendous path of risk and danger. And here was John, who was at the very end of the line, ready to let go."* And then their two worlds collided, and everything changed. Now she was sitting with her arms wrapped around this desperate boy who wanted to end it all. Mary closed her eyes as she tried to shut out the terrible things he must have endured to have driven him to this. The dreadful things that almost pushed her over the edge herself.

Then, Mary's thoughts turned a corner. All the unhappiness, misery, and pressure she had been enduring for so long had led to this night. Mary cringed a little inside as she thought of only hours earlier, when she had laid on her bed, drinking wine and crying with such bitterness. Then she got dressed in these clothes and put on terrible makeup, and she decided to find her way to McMurphy's Bar. But then her behavior in the cab had been so appalling and unhinged that the driver had kicked her out in the right spot at the right time. Because all those events lined up as perfectly as they could have, Mary saved this young man's life. Mary didn't understand how the impossible had just happened.

There must have been a point to it all. If Mary hadn't achieved something for the rest of her life, she would always have saved a life. She felt like a hero, but deep down, she realized she wanted to feel this way more often. She wanted to help people. She had literally pulled this poor boy back from the brink of something terrible—a catastrophic event. She could be tagged as a savior.

Mary mentally examined herself. Her feet were sore and bleeding, and her body was aching and cold. But her soul? Her spirit? Her heart? They all seemed to be filled with life and purpose. The energy Mary had wasted worrying about her father and carrying all that pain from that one night all those years ago, her no-good boyfriend suddenly seemed like a pitiful thing. Even now, as the ever-present vacuum left by her mother's death and her father's abominable mistake gnawed at her, it wasn't the sharp, unbearable feeling it often had. For some reason, the hope she had just found served as a balm for her broken heart. There was room for light now.

Leaning on the shoulder of the woman who had saved his life, John might as well have been in a dream. He felt certain that this person understood him and that he was right to feel closer to her than anyone else in the world. Not just because she had pulled him back from the fringes of death but because she had stayed with him, unquestioningly holding him and making everything feel alright.

John felt as though his heart had not just broken but had shattered into smithereens that lay around his chest in painful, wretched shards. He had so much to do in life and so much to say to the people in it. If it weren't for this woman, he would not be here. She had come running out of the darkness, throwing herself towards him, holding him, and screaming at him to live, to live, to live. Her words had pierced his intent, and he recalled that feeling when she was trying to pull him back from the brink, rising like a deep-sea diver to the surface of reality.

The two of them sat holding onto one another in the back of the cab, a curiously comfortable silence enveloping them. Both had thought life was hopeless and that there was nothing in their future except misery. Only by finding each other were they able to see that there was a sliver of hope. The world moved past the cab's window as it continued along the wet roads. Both John and Mary were silently starting to understand that the sun did not just rise in the morning for the benefit of other people; it rose every single morning for them as well. There was a shift in the fabric of time. Neither of them knew what it was, but anticipation swept through both of them. There was so much more for them. So much more... and they couldn't

138

wait to see what was waiting for them after this fateful night on the bridge.

16
SLIVER OF HOPE

Such is resilience of that one plant
pushing through the concrete
Daring to live against all odds

I just wanted the pain to stop. I just tried to make it stop. John didn't think that the enormity of that fact would ever diminish. And yet this woman had appeared on the bridge, at the very split second she could, to save his life. Could it be true that God's eye was indeed upon him? Had she been sent like an angel? She was barefoot and dirty with the rainwater from puddles. John didn't care for her identity; he just clung tighter and tighter to her as though he had never known physical comfort in his life.

Of all his longings, the desire to feel as though he belonged somewhere, with someone, was possibly the strongest. And now he was being held as though he mattered, as though he were loved, but by someone who didn't even know his name.

In an unwanted memory flash, he remembered falling off his bike once when he was a little boy and hurting his knee and his forehead badly. He remembered how warm he felt inside as his mother became genuinely worried about him, if only briefly, but the affection was there. She had drawn him against her on the big, brown sofa and held him in the crook of one arm while the other hand gently smoothed his hair back. She had lowered her mouth to his head and whispered, *"Shhh... shhh..."* to her youngest son's muffled cries. John clearly remembered that feeling of complete security and love, as he quickly forgot his hurts, snuggled there in his mother's arms. That memory made John warm inside and gave him mixed feelings as he had to remember that he had lost that warmth from his mother.

After that, John frequently pretended to be more badly hurt than he actually was in order to try to extract that love from his mother again. He had felt so safe and loved next to her like that, but it didn't happen again that he could recall, despite his attempts to engineer it. Eleanor Ribeaux had never been an affectionate woman with her children, but John wondered for the first time if she had her reasons. A jolt of horror struck him; if this woman had reached him a moment later, John would never have had the chance to find out. He could try to understand his mother more. Maybe in that alone, there would be hope for him to feel like he belonged in his own family.

The cab finally pulled up alongside the pavement of John's house—the same house he had fled from just hours earlier, seeking to end his own life. The atmosphere was pregnant with silence and many unsaid words. John and Mary felt cocooned in the car, like they were somehow safe and that time didn't affect them. They could exist at the moment and not worry about the next part—what would happen once the world rushed in at them again.

141

Joe looked at these two young faces and sighed inwardly. These kids shouldn't be battling so much pain; it wasn't right. He remembered how strung out the girl had been when he first picked her up at her house and the terrible and fraught behavior she had exhibited during the aborted drive to McMurphy's Bar. Whatever it was that had them both sitting on that bridge in the pouring rain was big and overwhelming for them both. His heart felt heavy for them. Joe saw life as a bright and wonderful thing, full of possibilities and wonder. He always believed and wanted to show others that life is a beautiful thing. How come these two had been passed by? How come they had so much to deal with that they sobbed as though their hearts were broken all the way from the bridge?

Joe remembered that, in the past, he had faced the same kind of darkness as them and taken the same walk. Joe felt a strange pang of emotion in his heart. Was it the pressing realization or acknowledgment that he left it to his wife to worry about the kids' mental state, and he just went out and earned money? How would he even know if something made his children sad or disturbed? If something was pushing them to the point that these two kids in his car had reached.

Joe shook his head as he started thinking about his own family. He remembered that, in the past, he had done everything to pay more attention to his children and to make his wife happy. Now, he seemed to have forgotten all about that. Now, all he did was save other people and make them happy. Joe regretted not being able to strike a balance between this newfound purpose and his family life. Yes, these people needed him, but so did his family. *"Remember to live again,"* he said to himself.

Moments later, a further pause followed, and Joe heard the girl start to move in the back of the car. Joe got out of the cab and went to open the door for his young passengers. Mary scrambled for her purse and began to count some cash with shaky hands. Then she realized she had no idea how much the fare was and lifted her eyes to Joe. He saw how exhausted she looked—frail and tear-stained.

"How much do I owe you?" Mary's voice was quiet and flat, and it seemed distant.

Joe shook his head. "This is on me. No charge. I hope you and that young man feel better soon. You can't lock up that darkness that's inside of you. You need to take it out of that vault. Stop protecting it. Choose every day to let go of it. Even when you think your actions are little, continue to chip away at the darkness until it dissipates. Choose to be happy against all odds. That's what I did." Joe turned around and started to walk away. As though remembering something crucial, he paused and turned back. "Remember that everything always gets better; no matter what you kids are going through, it will surely get better. Pain goes away; it's temporary. Once it's gone, then happiness can come back to take its place. The sun always rises." Mary had now caught up to him, so he gently took her hand, which was still offering the money, and closed her fingers around the dollars, keeping his hand on hers for a brief moment. "When happiness comes, hold on to it with your dear life. You can always make the pain go away, and you can bring happiness back. You really can."

Mary felt her lips tremble at the cab driver's unexpected wisdom and kindness. She stared at his worn, friendly face and felt a tear slip down her cheek. She smiled for the first time in what seemed so long and murmured, "Thank you. Thank you so much."

Joe walked a few feet to open the driver's door to the cab, which had taken Mary to and from the most pivotal moment of her life, and started to climb in. "You're welcome."

Mary turned to Joe and said, "I'm just going to make sure everything is fine with him, and if it's not too much trouble, can you take me home?" Joe gave Mary a grin. His heart felt a little lighter seeing the little smile touching her lips. Maybe things would work out for these kids after all. Joe watched Mary walk John up the stairs.

John stood next to her, his head down but at least now breathing calmly. *Once the pain has gone, happiness comes to take its place.* It seemed like such simple, homespun advice, yet, at the same time, it was profound and far-reaching. Mary could close her eyes and actually visualize the pain leaving, and in the void where the pain had been, light and hope came pouring in. She imagined herself letting go of the pain, the anger, the distrust, and the blame she had for her father, as well as the horror of that one night, which she had stored in her heart. *"I could do that. I can control those events. I can work through this pain."* Mary looked at John and put her arm around him. Rubbing his shoulder, she felt protective towards this young man she had met only a short time ago.

Mary felt something stir inside her. It was a swelling, fluttering feeling she dared to identify as something good— something bright and hopeful. Could this be the feeling of empowerment she had been searching for? Hope? Mary imagined herself taking hold of this feeling and cupping her hands around it. There was a small, warm spark within her, and if she was careful, she felt she could nurture it into life—a *spark to a flame.* Mary remembered a program on TV years ago about a tribe of nomads who kept a fire that never went out. They would keep a spark from the fire they had just used and continue to feed it religiously to keep it glowing. When they set up camp again, the spark would be blown against fresh tinder and kindling to create a new fire from the old one.

"A single spark could start a whole new fire. A whole new life with a fresh horizon," Mary closed her eyes at the thought. She recalled a speaker in one of her lectures talking about the seed of hope and happiness. All a seed needed to grow was light, soil, and water. Then a tiny seed, a mere speck in the hand, could become a beautiful, productive, living thing.

A single seed. Mary hugged the thought that she had that power within her, that single seed of hope. Despite everything, she couldn't help but break into a smile as she climbed into the cab.

~

John couldn't find the will or strength to raise his head. He heard the cab driver speak to Mary, saying something about pain making way for happiness or something. Then the cab door had closed, and the car was waiting to take Mary home. He knew Mary was right by him, and that at least gave him a little comfort.

He felt terribly confused, as though the events of the day had happened to someone else, almost. Things had seemed so clear before. He walked through in his head what he had done and where he had been, physically and emotionally. With a surge of understanding, he realized that he had experienced an almost complete mental and psychotic breakdown. He remembered reading a psychology book when he wanted his college major to be in psychology. It had referred to that very term, and now he felt as though jigsaw pieces had been suspended in mid-air, chaotically and frantically spinning around him, suddenly falling to the ground and into place, making the picture he had not been able to see before.

"I just wanted to be happy. I didn't want any more pain." The thought was clear as glass in John's mind. And then a stronger, surer thought hit him like a punch to the head: *"I want to live. I want to stay here. I want to LIVE."* John drew a deep breath into his lungs and then exhaled. The breath that left him felt like the first breath of the rest of his life. He felt like a newborn drawing its first breath. He could feel the unhappiness inside him begin to untangle itself from his soul, and as he breathed out, John could imagine that breath carrying with it the misery and sadness that had consumed him for so long.

Just then, he felt the gentle yet reassuring arm of the woman who had saved his life settle around his shoulders. Her grip was not firm, but it was as real and comforting as anything John could remember. He warmed inside, despite his cold, wet skin and clothes, as he thought of how she had appeared, almost flying towards him—not like Superman, but like Superwoman. His beautiful guardian angel had emerged from the darkness, and now she stood by him, still watching over him. Mary's face was thoughtful, and her gaze was distant. He couldn't read her thoughts, but they consumed her as she gazed into the distance. Still staring out of the window, Mary suddenly smiled a joyful, soft smile, so unexpectedly and unselfconsciously. John watched her, unbeknownst to Mary, as her face broke into the sweetest, most joyous smile.

There had been nothing to lift the desperate unhappiness and chaos of the night until that moment. The smile that lit Mary's face was a revelation, and somehow the power of it found John, and incredibly, he found that he, too, was smiling. A cautious, slightly bashful smile, but a smile nonetheless.

What was the reason this woman had found him? "I have never seen her before in my life," thought John, "yet there she was, just at the moment I needed her." In that dark night of cars speeding past and people rushing about their business, she somehow found him.

Had she sensed his overwhelming desire to end it all? Had she, by some incredible means, managed to feel his agony during those terrible moments on the bridge? Had something flown to her in the wind? Or like a predator, a shark maybe, sensing that somewhere, out of sight, there was blood in the water?

Even though he entertained the prospect of it, John couldn't help believing that maybe, just maybe, he wasn't meant to leave the world yet. Maybe there was a future for him after all. All the things that pulled him down—the depressive nature of his environment—weren't forever. Not forever. Things could change, and they would. Hadn't they changed when his guardian angel appeared? Maybe her materialization in his world was supposed to show him that he did deserve some happiness after all. Maybe there were things in his future that he was supposed to achieve, places he was meant to see, and people he was supposed to meet.

John lifted his head. *"Maybe she has been sent to make me understand that my journey might be hard and that there are demons that I have to fight, but I can do it. I can escape the depression and anxiety; one day, happiness will be mine for the taking."*

For the first time in so long, the heaviness that had dragged on his heart began to subside. John still felt a weight upon him, but this time he knew he could bear it. It wouldn't crush him. It would never crush him again, nor did it have power over him anymore.

They continued to stand there in front of his house. Litter danced and blew along the sidewalks, and what seemed like a forest of "To Let" signs leaned against the wind in front gardens. The old house looked well cared for, with pleasantly planted flowers out front, but they stood out rather than blended in.

John snapped out of his thoughts to see that the lights in his home were still on. The sight of the familiar jolted John back to the reality of his situation. There would be questions, maybe recriminations, and perhaps even tears. John knew he had to face it, but the idea made his body stiffen and shrink inside. But he had faced so much tonight. He had walked into the chaos of a terrible night and came through the other side. Whatever happened now didn't matter. But he squared his shoulders and began to walk towards the house, ready to face whatever came for him.

17

THE RETURN

The thread however tiny,
Tugs and tugs,
Leading to one place that is home

John knew that the girl was with him as he approached the door. A brand-new blue vehicle was parked outside the building, shining sleekly in the rain. This particular car had traversed a particular bridge this particular night, and although the familiarity ticked away at John's mind, he couldn't place why at first. He mulled over that pesky there-and-not-there memory at the edges of his mind and briefly returned to that moment on the bridge. He recalled that this was the same car that sped past him.

The two of them arranged themselves almost shyly on the step, bedraggled and exhausted as they were, and John placed his hand on the doorknob, ready to turn it quietly, assuming his mother was asleep or even awake, angrily pacing the floor in despair over her youngest son's disappearance.

As he touched the cool metal of the knob, the door swung open with such ferocity that the hinges tore at the wood in the frame. The door smashed against the wall, unnoticed by Eleanor Ribeaux, as she rushed out of the door and clutched her boy to her chest. She let out a deep, whiny, rumbling wail that John had never heard before. It was the noise that mothers—both human and animal—all over the world have made since time immemorial, the sound of agonized love that mothers have for their young. A lost child came back home.

Sobs shook his mother's body, and she poured her tears onto his head and into his hair. Her arms held him like a python wrapped around its prey, but there was no hostility in the embrace, and John knew it. He felt his body relax, and he slowly brought his arms up, wrapped them around her body, and held his mother back. When Eleanor felt her son's arms around her, her sobs became heavier as they racked her frame thoroughly, and fresh tears coursed down her face.

John buried his face in his mother's hair and cried with her. Instant emotion took over and overwhelmed him. "I'm so sorry, mom. I'm so sorry." His voice broke with tears and breathlessness. "I'm here. I'm sorry. I'm so sorry, mom." It seemed like hours passed while they stood there, hugging and crying together and wordlessly feeling the ebb and flow of love between them. John's eyes blurred with tears, but after a few moments, he noticed another figure in the room. Sean, his big brother! John felt his breath quicken and his heart thud with shock. *"Sean? Sean was here?"* He had uprooted himself from his busy life to check on his little brother. John could barely believe that his big brother was here; Sean actually cared enough to be here. Had he made all that effort for him? John squeezed his fingers onto his eyes to clear them, and just then, his brother came over and joined in the embrace, wrapping his long arms around his mother and little brother.

Eventually, Eleanor let go and held John's face between her hands, looking deeply into his eyes. "No, John, I should be saying sorry to you. All of this, it's all my fault. I should have been a better mother to you. To all of you." John opened his mouth to interrupt her, but she softly put a finger to his lips. "John, it's the truth. I didn't know where you were. You didn't come home. You didn't come home to me. I knew, my son. I knew that something was wrong. When I saw your note, I was heartbroken. I felt it here," she said, placing his hand on hers, which sat over her thumping heart. "The thought of losing you... I could not even bear it. You know I try to be a good mom, right? I had to try for all of you. I guess I failed at that for you boys, but especially for you, John. You needed me, and I wasn't there for you. I can't believe I didn't see the pain that you were going through."

His mother cupped her hands over her eyes and continued. "When I went out looking for you today, I felt like the darkness you were carrying became mine. I was tearing through the streets, looking for you. I ran out of gas twice," she continued, laughing hysterically. "I just couldn't stop looking. I couldn't stop. I was so scared, John. I was so worried." Eleanor stopped and let out a shuddering sigh. "Thank God you came back to me, thank God."

John suddenly remembered seeing his mother's uncharacteristic driving this morning and how he had noticed her speeding, which she never did. She had heartlessly driven past him, but it wasn't heartless at all. He realized that she had been out looking for him and was highly distraught and inattentive to her surroundings at the time. A lump formed in his throat. His mother had been worried about him. More importantly, his mother deeply loved him.

Eleanor held her youngest son to her chest again. "I tried; I really tried to be a better mother. It just seemed like every time things got better, something would happen, and life was hard again. I could barely keep our heads above water half the time." She closed her eyes and stroked John's head. "I thought we were doing okay—just surviving. I never had time or energy for the important stuff—love, attention, and kindness. I'm so sorry, John. I was spending so much time just trying to support the family that I didn't think to check in with you."

Eleanor nestled John's head against her and kissed his forehead. "Most of all, I should have told you I love you. I'm so, so proud of you."

John felt as though all of his prayers were being answered. How long had he wanted to be held like this—to feel loved? He needed her love and her guidance for so long. He needed it.

And now, here they were, finally holding each other, and he heard those words. "She's proud of me. She loves me. She really is proud of me. Someone is."

Somehow, the little family group had moved toward the heart of the house and was in the alcove between the kitchen and the living room. Sean held his arm around John, but it wasn't how he had done so before—as a way of wrestling him to the ground and yelling harsh words at him. It was a hug from his older sibling, and John felt safe. "I love you, little brother. Everything is going to be okay. We are here for you."

John looked at Sean, unsure of what he had just heard. Sean grinned and said again, "I love you, John. I love you, and I'm proud of you too." He kissed his little brother's forehead and rubbed his eyes.

Eleanor and John murmured their agreement. Then Sean held up his hand. "Before we go in, I think John should see something." With a kind, encouraging smile, which swiftly turned into great excitement and anticipation, Sean held the opened letter from Rumyph University towards John.

Eleanor clasped her hands together and let out a small cry. "Of course! I can't believe I nearly forgot. Oh, John, I'm excited for you to see this. I can't wait to see your face." She smoothed back her hair and laughed shakily. She had a smile like Sean's all over her face, filled with anticipation and happiness for something about to happen.

Suddenly, John was back in that dark, desperate place before his long walk to the bridge. Fear and sadness grabbed his chest, and he trembled and felt the panic rising inside him. "No, no, no... why did you open that? Why would you do that?"

Sean held his shoulder and smiled with love and warmth. Softly, in a voice of compassion and gentleness that John hadn't heard from his brother before, Sean spoke to John. "Please trust me. Open the letter and read it."

John shook his head and took the letter. Just holding the corner of the envelope made him feel distressed, and he could feel his breaths coming in short, sharp gasps. He looked at his mother, who had sat down on the sofa and was watching him and nodding gently.

Eleanor peered at the doorway and smiled warmly at the girl standing there, awkwardly fidgeting and tugging at her clothes while awkwardly shifting from one foot to the other. The girl had the most striking features, haunted by her own troubles. Eleanor recognized that frazzled, exhausted look in her eyes. She had been there once. John glanced at the girl with gratitude and respect gleaming in his dark eyes. Eleanor didn't understand completely, but she knew that this girl with her haunted eyes was the reason her boy was home with her. She beckoned Mary over to the sofa and gently took the girl's hand as she looked over to John. He nodded sheepishly.

Mary was grateful to be brought into the fold. She squeezed her fingers very slightly in appreciation of Eleanor. She wondered about her parents and how they would react in this situation. Mary briefly found herself shifting between two realities. In one, she saw the truth: John's mother was in front of her, and in the other, she imagined her late mother holding her. Somehow, it was easier to imagine her dead mother's reaction than her living father's. He would probably yell at her for causing all that trouble. She frowned slightly. Maybe he wouldn't yell. Perhaps he would be just as happy.

John remembered how the girl had saved him. He had a guardian angel of his own. He didn't need to be scared anymore. His mother and brother loved him. His hands trembling, John took the letter from the envelope. The paper was thick and expensive. It unfolded with the ease of something well-made.

We would like to congratulate you on being accepted into the School of Psychology for the semester commencing... John didn't read anymore. He looked at his mother's glowing, proud face; the smiling, loving face of his brother; and finally, that of Mary, who had watched this beautiful family scene unfold and had guessed that the envelope must contain good news.

John smiled at these beloved faces. His smile came from deep within him and was a flag of his joy and happiness, which had bloomed within him. He looked back down at the letter, which he now gripped firmly in each hand, and read on. "Look at the second page, bro," Sean said, interrupting his train of thought. John did as he was instructed and read. The letter was not the standard acceptance but a personal message from the School of Psychology's Department Chair. John read on in awe, amazed at how his life had shifted by so many degrees in such a short time.

...and so, I want to take this opportunity to write to you personally, which I rarely do, so that I may offer my deepest and most sincere congratulations upon being accepted into this great institution.

The essay you submitted in support of your application was one of the most accomplished and inspiring accounts of a student's ambitions that I have read in many years. Your explanation of your personal struggles was articulate and moving.

Indeed, you are right. Many other people suffer around the world, and resources to help them should be improved and extended to all who need them. Your desire to eventually gain your Ph.D. and then go on to establish an organization to help young people through the distress of mental illness and help them recover is aligned with my own deeply held ambitions.

I have great admiration for your determination to not only conquer your obstacles but also help others conquer theirs. It is with this in mind that I took the liberty of personally recommending you for this scholarship. With utmost delight, I am happy to inform you that the committee has proudly named you the recipient of the Irene & Gianna-Louise Waters Scholarship. This, as you may know, comes with additional grants that will meet the cost of your college education and additionally provide funding for your non-profit organization in its early years.

John blinked once. He blinked again. What?! He folded the letter silently and then unfolded it. He shook his head in disbelief. New tears sprung to his eyes, but these were purely tears of joy. He was at home, loved, and safe, and now he had a future—a wonderful, exciting future.

He imagined himself on the bridge again, cold, wet, and alone, desperately sad and without hope. Now he had all the things that he had dreamed of. John felt like the luckiest, happiest person alive that night. If Mary hadn't saved him, he never would have known how much he was loved and valued. He had been delivered into the love and approval he had needed so desperately. "*I had no idea,*" John thought, "*no idea how loved I am.*"

He hugged his mother, his brother, and Mary close to him. Nothing could shake the shining happiness that had found him, which he now embraced so tightly. Suddenly, now that he was safe and home, he felt the bone-deep exhaustion his intense emotions had kept at bay.

There were no words for everything that John felt. He turned, almost shyly, to his mother and brother. "Thank you, both of you. Thank you for..." John's voice broke a little with emotion. "Thank you for your love. Thank you for caring about me." He assured himself that he wasn't dreaming. His eyes met Mary's, and instant joy filled his heart. He was so grateful to meet someone who understood him without words. "I hope you don't mind, but I'm pretty exhausted." As he spoke, his brother put an arm around him, sensing his little brother's weariness and need for rest. John looked at Sean gratefully. "I think I need to turn in. It's been a long night."

Eleanor nodded, her eyes shining with tears and love. The beaming mother, weary with worry and now buzzing with relief, was looking to make some tea. As she did, John stepped toward Mary, who rose to meet him. John couldn't think of the right words. He suddenly felt that the right words hadn't been invented for what he needed to say to Mary. But he had a feeling she would understand that, and his failure to find the words didn't mean that his feelings didn't run as deep as the ocean. He embraced Mary, his eyes closed, knowing that this young woman would always be part of his life somehow. She had given him all her meaning back. He would never forget it.

Mary hugged him back, and they were like that for a minute. It felt like they were communicating with each other without words. After the heartfelt embrace, they nodded to each other with small smiles before John disappeared through the staircase.

Sean had been watching how his little brother and the young lady who had shouted at him on the road earlier communicated without words. He felt slightly jealous and bad that he could not be there for his baby brother. All the same, he was grateful for his life.

As Sean was about to acknowledge Mary, Eleanor walked in with two mugs of hot tea. She looked around and noticed that John had left. A little part of her wanted to go and tuck him in, but she knew he needed his space. She offered Mary tea, but she turned it down.

"Please take some. It's the least I could do to express my gratitude for bringing John back to us," she said, her voice breaking. Mary reluctantly took the tea as she stared at the front door. She didn't want to keep Joe waiting, but she couldn't dismiss a mother's request. After taking some tea, she dropped the mug on the table beside her.

Instantly, Eleanor took Mary's hand and looked deeply into her eyes. "Thank you," Eleanor mouthed, clasping the girl's hand. "Thank you." Mary smiled softly and returned the squeeze with her fingers, nodding in acknowledgment of Eleanor's feelings.

Trying to hold back her tears, Eleanor smiled as they rolled down her cheeks. "I don't know what happened out there, but I know that you brought my son back. I don't know what I would have done. I don't know... You brought my son back to me. You brought my son back... You didn't just save him; you saved us all," a sob interrupted her words, but she carried on, nevertheless. "I can never, ever thank you enough. This is now your home too. We will welcome you with open arms, come rain, come sunshine. You are family," Eleanor said. She hugged Mary for a brief moment, and the two women smiled at each other.

Sean stared at his mother and saw how tired she looked. "Why don't you turn in now? You're tired, and you need to rest." He said as he placed his hand on her back.

She returned his gesture with a small smile as she turned to face Mary, "Goodnight, my dear. Thank you once more, and don't hesitate to stop by anytime. I owe you that much."

Eleanor said to Mary as she crossed the room and went up the stairs, leaving Mary and Sean standing alone in the sitting room, both looking a little relaxed at the whole incident. There was so much ahead for them—all of them.

18
THE PAIN DISAPPEARS

The dark pregnant clouds
Looming over the city
Suddenly begin to clear
For the first time in forever, I see the sun

Sean grinned and went to introduce himself properly, but as he did, Mary began to cry. Sean was surprised at first, but then he understood immediately.

"I guess you've had a pretty rough night as well."

Mary began to nod and unexpectedly found more hot tears rushing through her eyes. She was too exhausted to stop them. She cried for herself, John, and this family that had found each other again. Suddenly, it felt like the barricades she had so carefully spent decades building around herself had been blown right through. Mary had built a shell around herself, and everyone believed that she was so in control, but inside, she felt so weak and lacking in her self-worth. She felt safe in his arms, but she remembered that Joe was still waiting for her patiently outside. She broke free from his warm hug and said, "Sorry, I have to catch my ride." Sean was confused since Mary had been inside their house for a while. When their eyes met, they knew they recognized each other from the bridge. Now that Mary wasn't screaming at him to leave her alone, she looked so different. He hoped to see her again. Through her sadness, he caught her beauty and wanted to hold her as she did to his brother. He caught her hand as she walked to the door and asked for her number. Mary smiled tiredly before giving him her number. She headed out, leaving Sean behind in the house.

Mary walked almost sluggishly to Joe's car as she sank into deep thought. She had never spoken of any of it before and was suddenly aware that she had been walking along an emotional high wire, getting bashed and knocked as she tried to keep her balance, and all of a sudden, she had quite simply had enough of it. She was no longer struggling to get to the other side, dragging her pain and unhappiness behind her. She had decided to leap off the high wire, jump down, and stop worrying about what it all meant. "Joe was a stranger," she thought as she continued her seemingly long trek to the car. She could pour it all on him; in any event, it seemed she couldn't stop herself from doing so. So far, he had shown he was a great and wise listener.

As Joe watched her figure through the rearview mirror, he was grateful that she was finally looking like her burdens had vanished, but he had more jobs to do, and she had been in the house for a while. "You've got to get moving, kid. I have more rides to complete tonight," Joe said to her, which made Mary walk faster toward the cab.

When she reached the vehicle, she swung the door open and plopped into the passenger seat in one fluid motion. Joe revved up the engine, and the journey started. The ride was quiet at first until Mary broke the silence. She spoke her heart out to Joe, and he listened as most cab drivers do. However, this was different from any conversation with the other cab drivers. He smiled as she talked, like he knew what was going on. He was proud of how she held herself together despite her troubled past. When she finally stopped talking, fresh tears rolled down her cheeks. She felt like a burden had been lifted from her chest. When her eyes met Joe's, she became slightly embarrassed about her outpouring. Joe grabbed a tissue and handed it to her. She wiped her eyes as he focused on navigating the road ahead.

"You know, I'm sure your mom is really proud of what you did tonight," Joe said as he exchanged glances with Mary briefly through the rearview mirror.

Mary nodded with a small smile as her mind wandered to the memories of her mother.

The drive became quiet until Mary noticed her phone ringing again. She just looked at her phone and turned it off. She had enough drama for a night and wasn't in the mood to answer any calls.

The night had been so long, and Mary remembered every detail of its events. She knew she could no longer go back home and continue being the same person she was. Deep down, Mary knew that something huge had changed in her. The epiphany was thick and heavy, hard to deny as it settled in her heart. After taking a deep breath, she finally got the strength to address the ominous statement he had made earlier on the bridge. After all, it had been one of the few things that had occupied her mind since she saved John on the bridge.

"So, I think I understand what you meant when you said find someone to take care of."

"You do, now?" Joe immediately answered, unsure if she knew what the future had in store for her. "Thank God you understand. Sometimes we go through things just so that we can have enough strength to help others going through them. Understanding them is easier when you've been in that exact position. I'm glad you were just in time to save that boy. I knew he would be there, and he would need your help." Mary's breath caught in her throat as her eyes widened in surprise. She swallowed before continuing the conversation.

"You knew that he was there? What do you mean, you knew he was there? How did you know he was there? How did you know I would help him?" The questions came tumbling out of Mary's mouth as she now looked at Joe with wary eyes.

"It's kind of hard to answer that question," Joe explained. "Something you can't explain. Everyone has been sent here with a purpose. I think your purpose is to help people. Actually, I know it is, and that's why I'm here to help you as you journey into this new purpose in your life." He chuckled softly.

Still wearily eyeing Joe, Mary wondered if now was the right time to jump out of the cab. Her eyes darted out of the window and onto the roadside briefly. Still, something compelled her to stay. Mary could not explain it, nor could she explain why, but there was this feeling, almost a conviction, that Joe was not here to hurt her. As ridiculous as it would have seemed to any sane person, she felt an odd sense of comfort with Joe even though the conversation took a weird turning point, a peculiar one at that. While her common sense screamed at her to bolt as fast as she could, Mary knew she would not do that. She couldn't. Hugging herself tightly with her arms wrapped around her torso, she gazed at the night sky through the window. She couldn't understand what Joe had just said.

How did he know so much about things that he could not possibly have known about? She leaned her head against the headrest and whispered, "Thank you for everything you have done tonight. I can't explain it, but thank you." Mary felt like she had purpose and clarity for the first time in forever.

Joe gave a wide grin as he turned into the gas station. "Hey, it's absolutely fine," he replied.

"Everything that has happened to you, to John, happened for a reason. Things happen, and we must battle ourselves, our beliefs, and our impulse to love, no matter what. We have to learn how to pick ourselves back up again." He glanced at Mary to see if she was listening to him. She was very intently absorbing every piece of advice he had for her. "Everyone has their own journey in life, but as you can see, some of them just take the wrong road. All those things you go through are like waves, pushing you and moving you toward your destination. Sometimes the waves are huge and crash down on top of you. Sometimes, they're ripples, calmly guiding you through the currents so gently that you hardly know that you're moving. At the end of the day, everything will be fine."

Mary stared, her mouth slightly agape with wonder. It made sense—everything that came out of Joe's mouth. He was such a good storyteller. "Wow!" she silently exclaimed.

Joe smiled a little awkwardly, given the events of the night. "Yeah, I guess that about covers it. Also, the pain goes away eventually, and, in its place, happiness arrives."

Mary looked at him in agreement. "Yes. Yes. I think you're right," she murmured and smiled softly.

Mary was lost in her thoughts for a few moments, thinking about how she had learned more about herself in one night than she had over the years. Everything happens for a reason. She was stronger and more positive than she had ever been before. Her entire life lay ahead of her just from this night and beyond. And it would be good and bad, but she could handle it. She could handle the rest of the night and tomorrow as well.

As Joe opened the door to fill the car with gas, Mary's stomach rumbled, reminding her that she'd had very little to eat.

"Joe, I'll be right back; I just want to get a late-night snack at the minimart," she said as she got down from the cab.

"I'm so proud of you," Joe smiled. Shocked at his confession, she looked at him.

Joe turned to Mary and said, "Well, I guess it's time."

Mary assumed he meant it was time for him to take her home, so she told him to give her a second and ran to the nearby store.

"I love you, May," Joe whispered. Mary froze in her tracks. She was sure she heard him say that he loved her. Even more confusing was the fact that the only person who called her May was her mother. Ready to ask him about it, Mary decided against it when she looked back at Joe. With his hands still loosely hanging off the wheel, he looked deep in thought. Perhaps she had imagined him saying it; it had been a long night. Mary walked towards the store briskly but stopped in her tracks as she put her hand on the door and pulled gently. Joe's words, or at least what she thought he said, still bugged her. She turned back to look at the car.

A cold gust of wind swirled around Mary, giving her goosebumps. In the seconds it had taken her to cross to the door, the car and Joe had completely vanished. Shaking her head in disbelief and blinking furiously, she scanned the parking lot for her new friend, searching the empty lot. There had been no engine sound, and no cars had driven past—where was Joe?

Running to the edge of the road, she scanned left and right; there was no way Joe could have left and been out of sight in those few seconds.

"Joe? Joe?" She yelled but received no response. She was confused about how he could just vanish. With her hands on her head as she turned around, eyes darting back and forth in a frenzy. How did he just disappear like that? Still hyperventilating, Mary shook her head as though to shake off this crazy hallucination. This whole thing was surreal, confusing, and frightening. Something nearly convinced her that she was never really there.

Everything had changed tonight for Mary. She started the day feeling powerless, unable to grasp any future for herself apart from continuing to reach for perfection, even though it had eluded her throughout her life. The bridge had changed it all. She had lost herself completely on that bridge, and running to save that boy from following through on a dark decision had left her feeling so much hope as she continued to follow the unknown road. However, at that moment, she felt lost and confused. The world started to spin around Mary. It felt like she would lose her balance and topple over like a figurine placed on a wobbly shelf.

She looked down at the spot where the cab was parked before it disappeared along with Joe. Something glinted in the light from the ground, and she crossed to where the car had stood, feeling crazy, confused, and bewildered. Stooping closer to inspect the object catching the light, she gasped. A familiar necklace lay in the spot where Joe had sat—a necklace that bore an eerie resemblance to her mother's favorite. It couldn't be. Mary hadn't seen the necklace since she lost it years ago when she left home for school. With her hands trembling in doubt, confusion, and fear, she picked it up to check if it had her mother's initials engraved on it. Mary had no idea she had been holding her breath until she saw the initials. There they were. Those three letters gave Mary solace when she needed it the most.

Frozen in shock at the odd discovery, Mary clutched the necklace and pressed it to her heart. The tears easily slipped out of her eyes, spilling down her cheeks and gathering at her chin. A bright light beaming down from above harshly pressed on her face, forcing her to open her eyes, which were squeezed shut.

When Mary looked up through squinted eyes, the light was hot, bright, and burning. As the light seared on her eyes, it started to dim enough for her to see that there was something—or rather, someone—up there. The clouds, still bruised from the storm, rolled in the sky, shifting and troubled. But along with the dazzling light shafts, they had formed an obvious shape to Mary, so familiar that she pressed the heels of her palms into her eyes, rubbing furiously. A glowing figure, serene and calm against the battered sky, watched down over Mary. Even though she could hardly see, there was no mistaking the blurry outline that she saw. She was entranced by the spectacle above her. The air felt charged with electricity, stronger than any storm could bring. The hairs on Mary's body stood on end, and she felt peaceful and serene. She knew who that was. "Mom?" she called out in a cracked voice, searching the sky for answers. It was then that she heard her mother's voice. It drifted into her consciousness from the edge of her mind. Warm like hot cocoa and smooth like silk, Elise Hart said the last words Mary heard before everything went black: "May, sweet May. If you can hear me, I love you and miss you. Come back to me."

19
THE SECOND CHANCE

In every bad situation
Life gives you a second chance
To make it right
Some take it, Others leave it
And most don't see it

The beeping of an unknown machine was the first thing Mary heard before opening her eyes. An antiseptic smell then drifted through her senses. Opening her eyes proved to be a difficult task in itself. Her eyelids were heavy and thick, like they had been shut for too long and did not know how to open anymore.

When Mary finally forced her eyes open, they slammed shut almost immediately as the unbelievably bright, harsh lights beamed on them. She must have left the blinds open when she got home. Home? She didn't remember getting home. Too tired to try and open her eyes again, Mary internally groaned at the white-hot pain searing through her head. Above that pain, a duller ache spread throughout her body. Mary had never been this tired before, she thought, as she noted how parched her mouth and throat were. It must have been the aftereffects of the drinking and the crazy events of her night with Joe and John. Mary laid in bed, hoping to stay there for a little longer. With her eyes closed, she started to replay everything that had happened the night before. Goodness, that was a crazy night. "*I need to get up. God knows how long I've been asleep,*" Mary thought with a hint of vigor. Her mind felt renewed and sharpened, and despite the pain and tiredness in her body, she felt ready to take on the new day. She felt like a new, more powerful person, stronger than ever before. This drum of excitement started to tank when her mind played the events of yesterday in her mind. Confusion washed over her once more as she found herself back in the parking lot of that small grocery store, confused because Joe had vanished. Mary heard the same unknown machine beep even faster somewhere in the distance of her consciousness. Her mouth, "*ergh,*" and her tongue felt like sandpaper; she needed water.

With more determination—especially to shut off that machine—Mary forced her eyes open again, this time slowly to allow them to adjust to the stark white light.

Mary could feel her eyes watering as her thoughts swam sluggishly in her head. She slowly realized that she didn't remember coming back home. In fact, she didn't remember anything from the point when Joe mysteriously disappeared into thin air. Confusion set in heavily as she shut her eyes again and fought hard to remember what happened afterward.

The necklace. Mom's necklace. Remembering the necklace quickly thrust Mary back into the memory of being in the parking lot. Joe and the car were gone, and she was staring into a bright light above her, looking at a silhouetted figure of her mother in the sky. Was it a ghost? Was it an angel? Was she hallucinating?

Instinctively, Mary curled up the hand she had held the necklace in. The necklace was there, alright, but so was a warm hand. Mary panicked instantly. Why was there someone in her house? Her eyelids were too heavy as her eyes darted back and forth behind them. What was happening? Where was she? The hands slipped from Mary's weak hold as a woman's voice screamed, "Oh my God, Gray."

Mary was almost certain she was hallucinating and imagining things at this point. There was no mistaking that voice. It was her mother's voice.

Mary froze in her bed, almost afraid to open her eyes. What is going on? There was a lot of ruffling around as the same woman started sobbing in the distance as though she had moved away. A door swung open and slammed shut somewhere in the distance. All of this was too much! Mary's head started to swim.

The beeping of the machine suddenly picked up somewhere not too far off. Confused even more, Mary slowly peeled her eyes open. She wasn't met by the cold, white ceiling like she was the first time she opened her eyes. She found herself staring into warm, brown eyes that were widening in surprise. It was John.

John?

What was John doing in her house?

Mary struggled to ask John precisely that as she realized how dry and parched her mouth was. "John?" she managed to say instead. "Hey, you," John replied with a warm smile.

"What are you doing here? What is going on?" Mary asked. John's expression softened as he held Mary's hand in his large, warm hands. "Please relax, Mary. It's a long story. So much has happened, Mary." So much has happened? What did he mean? Why was he here? The questions would not stop tumbling around in Mary's head, although she was too weak and dehydrated to speak. "Let mom and dad come back with the doctor. They'll explain everything."

"Mom? Doctor? What is going on?" The question seemed excessively repeated at this point, but so was Mary's confusion.

Mary's eyes darted to the door as it swung open, revealing two people she most certainly did not expect to see. There she was: Elise Hart in all her beautiful glory, looking like she had not aged a single day. Even though she was dressed in a simple dress with stress telling on the lines across her forehead, the woman was still as perfect as she always was.

Mary briefly wondered if she was going crazy as her eyes slowly drifted to her father. Beside Elise was Grayson Hart, who was tall and intimidating. He was undeniably out of character, clad in sweatpants in place of his staple Armani suit. A growing beard shadowed his ever-clean-shaved face, and his eyes were saggy with dark bags underneath them.

"Mom?" Mary said in a confused whisper as her parents rushed to her, embracing her tightly. John immediately joined in on the hug. Mary's mother was sobbing again as she cradled Mary's head lovingly on her chest, pressing urgent kisses on the top of her head.

"My baby girl. My baby girl," Elise said as all three of them continued hugging a confused Mary.

"Mom? Dad? What... what happened? What's going on?"

The hug stopped as Elise wiped the tears from her face and perched beside her on the bed. She held Mary's face in her hands while John and Grayson stood beside Mary's bed, holding each of her hands gently.

"Honey, you had a bad fall. You've been in a coma for two months."

"Coma?"

"Yes, sweetheart. Oh, we were so scared," Elise said as she hugged her daughter again. "The doctor will be here soon." Doctor? Mary questioned herself as she focused harder on escaping this bizarre dream. A dream, that's what it had to be. None of this was real. It couldn't possibly be.

Unaware of her internal turmoil, Mary's mother hugged her gently again, kissing her forehead. Thoughts, both meaningful and otherwise, raced through Mary's mind. This had to be a really strange dream.

"Darling, we were so afraid you would never come back to us," Grayson said as he squeezed Mary's hand gently. This has to be the craziest dream ever.

"What's going on?" Mary parroted the question again as though everything they had said made no sense.

Elise sighed, looking behind her at her husband. Grayson Hart cautiously stepped towards Mary's bed, and when he did, he held her hand firmly in his. "My baby girl," his voice cracked as he bowed his head, sobbing.

Mary was in shock, to say the least. Her eyes darted back and forth as she looked around in utter confusion. "Mary," her mom said softly as she sighed deeply and started explaining.

"Your father and I... We had a fight and...."

The sound of breaking glass startled sleeping Mary awake! The fourteen-year-old groaned and tugged the blankets away, silently swinging her feet to the carpet.

"You need to watch your tone with me, Elise!" The raised voice penetrated the walls. The sound of shattering glass made its way to Mary's ears again.

"I'm the one who needs to watch my tone?" Elise spat, "That's rich coming from you. You're the one who made me the way I am. You know that, don't you?" There was a loaded silence as Mary braced herself to rise from bed soundlessly, leaving her puzzled over her next move in the stillness.

The door opened again to let out a continued stream of Elise's yelling, and Mary grimaced. "All you do is blame me for everything that goes wrong! All you do is act like you're a saint. I deserve better, Grayson!" Elise's voice had begun to crack from all the yelling by the time little Mary's body slipped out from under her pink covers.

"If this is another one of your nagging sprees, I'm not interested," her father heatedly replied. By now, Mary had settled in front of the door through which the shouting floated, debating what to do.

She peered through the keyhole into the room, holding her breath. There was a carry-on bag on the glorious king-sized bed that she had once loved to jump on—much to her mother's chagrin.

Clothes were strewn everywhere, some haphazardly shoved in the bag, while some barely made it over the top. Right by her mother's vanity, Mary's parents stood in front of each other. The girl could almost smell the hate and anger that permeated the air, like the thick smoke in the kitchen whenever her mom forgot she had something in the oven.

Her body began to ache from crouching at the door. Her heart was thumping like it never had before. Her palms started to sweat. Mary shakily took a deep breath as she watched her parents get into another round of their shouting match.

THE SECOND CHANCE

"You're such an ungrateful woman! You had better take those filthy clothes, put them where they need to be, and stop this nonsense, Elise. I don't have the time for this!"

Elise didn't pay much attention to her husband. She was too busy shoving at his looming figure to get to her carry-on bag. She was leaving. She couldn't deal with the fighting and the emptiness anymore. She was done.

Grayson grabbed his wife by the arm like a petulant child in need of a thorough spanking. He looked her dead in the eye. "I'm only going to say it once. You get that bag and those clothes back into the closet and go to fu— "

*Mary didn't see the slap, but she heard it, making her clap her hand to her mouth to disguise the sharp breath she drew. Loud and clear, **smack!** The girl watched her parents stare at each other in silence as though they were frozen in time. Her feet really hurt.*

"How dare you?" Grayson exclaimed as he grabbed Elise's arm even harder and shook her like one of Mary's raggedy dolls. That was the first time Mary ever saw her mother hit her father. She swallowed, torn between interrupting their latest spat and returning to her room and curling up in bed, buffered by her covers.

Grayson shoved Elise hard at the grand vanity in disgust while muttering the bad words Elise always cautioned him about when Mary was within range. Elise grunted as she collided headfirst with the vanity and fell in a heap beside it, the mirror shattering all over the dresser.

"When you're done with your pointless whining, you know what to do," Grayson muttered as he flung Elise's clothes onto the maroon rug beside his wife's form on the floor. Elise did not respond.

173

Silence.

"Get up, Elise. Enough with this; you'll wake Mary and John." Silence. Mary's heart felt like it might explode from her chest as she repeated her father's words in her mind, "Get up. Get up, please."

Grayson stopped flinging the clothes. With Elise's favorite green sequined dress in his hands, he stepped tentatively towards Elise as she lay on the rug. "Elise?" Elise remained quiet. In her terror, Mary's shaking hand instinctively reached for the doorknob.

Grayson turned her over and gasped sharply as the shimmering green dress fell from his trembling hands to the floor. "Elise, wake up!" He swore loudly and grabbed his phone to make a call, only to drop the phone, impatient to make a phone call and risk having to wait for help to get there. With tears blurring his vision, Grayson Hart gathered his wife's limp body in his arms and rushed to the door, where, unbeknownst to him, Mary stood on the other side, wide-eyed and pale as a ghost, still peeping through the keyhole. The girl hurried away before he turned the knob.

However, her escape was cut short when she slipped on the staircase. The fall was loud and painful. Mary had blacked out by the time she reached the bottom of the stairwell. She had hit her head badly on her fall, and blood was now gushing out of her head through a huge gash on the back of her head. She didn't hear her father yelling her brother's name, John. She didn't hear John rush to her at the bottom of the stairs to carry her small frame in his arms.

She didn't hear her father sobbing regretfully as they drove to the hospital in the rain. She didn't hear her big brother

174

repeatedly calling her name, begging her and her mother to stay with them. Mary had no idea what had happened.

What sort of dream is this? Am I going crazy?

"Oh no!" Mary exclaimed. Everyone instantly started to fuss over her. Was she feeling any pain? Was something wrong?

Mary slowly shook her head.

"I don't know what's going on," she whispered as she slowly raised her hands in front of her face. Those were not the hands of a 20-something-year-old lady. They were her hands— the hands of a teenager, hands that experimented with her mother's makeup with chipped neon nail varnish.

"What do you mean?" John said as he perched beside her on the bed. Mary shook her head as though she could shake off all the confusion. With a deep, defeated sigh, Mary said, "I... I had a... dream."

Elise nodded at her daughter, clasping her hands over hers and encouraging her to speak. Mary started slowly, fighting to speak through the lethargy that weighed down her senses. She told them that she had a bizarre dream that was, at some point, real to her. Scared to share the unpleasant details of that life with them, Mary did not say any more.

The family of four was suddenly yanked out of that intense moment when everyone's eyes darted to the door simultaneously as it swung open. A tall, dark-haired man in a white coat came breezing through. Grayson turned around and shook hands with the doctor who had walked to Mary's bed. John and Elise stepped back to let the doctor and Grayson get closer. He walked straight up to her bed and started a check-up.

"Hello, Mary. You've had quite an eventful past couple of months, haven't you? I'm sure your parents have told you all about it. You had a fall, and they brought you here to us. You have been asleep for quite a long time," he paused as he flashed a torch over her eyes, asking her to follow the light with her eyes. "We are glad to have you back."

Mary was absent-minded for most of the check-up, barely understanding what he said as she struggled to make sense of what was going on. Taking his eyes off her for a moment, the doctor stared at the machines around her intensely. Grayson softly spoke to the doctor, telling him that Mary had informed them of her dream while in the coma.

Mary could not believe it had all been a dream. She turned to John and said, "I dreamt that John... you... got into college at Rumyph University. It was all so real."

John's shock was hard to miss. He looked at their parents in disbelief. "Mary, I did get into Rumyph; how did you—"

Recalling Mr. Hart's revelation about his patient's coma dream, the doctor interjected, explaining to Mary's family. "If what Mary shared with us is true, then it is possible that she had moments in her coma when she was able to pick up bits of conversations being had around her. While this is uncommon, quite a considerable number of coma patients have been discovered to have been hearing what was happening around them," he paused.

"It is not surprising that Mary might have overheard you discussing this and, somewhere in her subconscious, added it to this unbelievably vivid dream of hers."

Dream.

It was all a dream.

Mary felt dizzy. "*I can't believe it was all a dream.*"

"Mr. and Mrs. Hart, can I speak to you outside for a moment?" the doctor finally said as he stepped outside, with Mary's parents following closely behind.

As they walked out, John squeezed Mary's hand. With tears in his eyes, he said, "Mary, everything you said happened in your dream... I think I felt it."

He then admitted that, ever since she fell into a coma, he had fallen into a very depressed state. Every night, he would come to talk to her about his struggles, from how the pressure at school was suffocating him to how worried he was about her.

"With all that was going on, I was so tired...so, so tired. I... I came in here one night to say goodbye. I was going to end my pain, Mary," he said as he burst into tears and hugged her tightly. "I was going to end my pain in the most horrible way, but the moment I sat beside you, I could swear I felt you hug me," he added as he sobbed quietly. "I couldn't do it. I couldn't leave. I didn't do it, Mary."

Elise and Grayson walked in to see their two children sobbing as they held each other. The parents joined them; all of them huddled over the small hospital bed, crying happy tears as Mary's doctor watched the heartwarming moment.

Eventually, Elise broke the silence. "Mary, the doctor would like to run some more tests. We'll be in the hallway, sweetie. I'm going home to get you a change of clothes and some food." She gave Mary a tight, warm hug and stepped aside for John and Grayson to hug her before they all left the room.

The doctor stepped forward to start the rest of the tests. "Well, Mary, it seems like you have had quite an interesting two months," he said lightheartedly with warm eyes.

Mary smiled.

"Your experience, although unique, is not strange at all. Many times, when patients like you go through this, they often take whatever their dreams show as a guide. Perhaps there was a message you needed to learn in that dream of yours," the doctor said as he continued poking and prodding at the machines around her.

Mary mulled over what he said.

Here she was, still fourteen years old, with her mother alive. Still, that dream was as vivid as real life. The doctor noticed how deep in thought she was and quickly added, "There's no need to be so bothered, Mary. It will take you a while to get adjusted to this reality again. We're just glad to have you back. Not many people come back after such a serious fall."

The doctor offered her another warm smile before telling her he was done. Finally, he said, "If you need anything, just reach out to me," and turned to walk away.

"Wait, doctor. You didn't tell me your name."

With a hand on the door, the doctor turned his head and answered. "My name is Dr. Yphrum. Joe Yphrum."

Mary stared at the back of his head, her mouth gaping.

He smiled knowingly again. "Well, I guess it's time. Take care of yourself, pretty lady, and find someone to take care of."

Mary's eyes widened like saucers as he walked out of the room.

Joe?

About the Author

Earl Brown has received numerous awards, accolades, and acknowledgments from the highest levels for his lifetime work in youth development, higher education, and community advancement. He has been a true champion of the continued improvement needs in our youth and communities, not only with respect to educational attainment and economic mobility but, very importantly, in mental health and wellness.

Earl lives in New Jersey with his wife, Maria, and is surrounded by his wonderful family and friends. From an early age, Earl started to volunteer his time with youth and community organizations, realizing the importance of giving back, which opened his eyes to the extreme issues many people face regarding education and mental health awareness.

Earl earned his bachelor's degree in Economics and Business Management from Virginia Tech University. He then went on to earn his M.B.A. from George Mason University. Earl's career experience has been in business, education, and community development.

Earl is most proud of his work in education and youth development, and he continues to be a champion for the advancement of our youth and the downtrodden in low-income communities.

If you want to know more about Earl Brown and his background, please visit his website at
www.EarlBrownEDU.com

Instagram: EarlBrownEDU
Email: EarlBrownEDU@gmail.com